"You're Going To [...] Child?" Katie Asked Cautiously.

"I spent most of the night thinking about it, and if you're agreeable, then yes, I'll help you."

"Agreeable? Just what would I be agreeing to?"

"I want joint custody," Jeremiah said. "This will be the only child I ever have. I intend to be part of his life."

Katie considered what he said. "I suppose we could work out—"

He held out his hand. "Before you agree, you'd better hear me out."

"You have more stipulations?" she asked incredulously.

"Just one."

"Why do I get the idea I'm not going to like your next demand?"

He shrugged. "You never know. You might enjoy it."

A fresh wave of goose bumps slid along her arms and every instinct in her being told her to turn and run as far and as fast as she possibly could in the opposite direction. Instead, she swallowed hard and asked, "What is it?"

Jeremiah nodded. "I'd make love to you until you became pregnant."

Dear Reader,

Yes, we have what you're looking for at Silhouette Desire. This month, we bring you some of the most anticipated stories…and some of the most exciting new tales we have ever offered.

Yes, *New York Times* bestselling author Lisa Jackson is back with Randi McCafferty's story. You've been waiting to discover who fathered Randi's baby and who was out to kill her, and the incomparable Lisa Jackson answers all your questions and more in *Best-Kept Lies*. Yes, we have the next installment of DYNASTIES: THE DANFORTHS with Cathleen Galitz's *Cowboy Crescendo*. And you can be sure that wild Wyoming rancher Toby Danforth is just as hot as can be. Yes, there is finally another SECRETS! book from Barbara McCauley. She's back with *Miss Pruitt's Private Life*, a scandalous tale of passionate encounters and returning characters you've come to know and love.

Yes, Sara Orwig continues her compelling series STALLION PASS: TEXAS KNIGHTS with an outstanding tale of stranded strangers turned secret lovers, in *Standing Outside the Fire*. Yes, the fabulous Kathie DeNosky is back this month with a scintillating story about a woman desperate to have a *Baby at His Convenience*. And yes, Bronwyn Jameson is taking us down under as two passionate individuals square off in a battle that soon sweeps them *Beyond Control*.

Here's hoping you'll be saying "Yes, yes, yes" to Silhouette Desire all month…all summer…all year long!

Melissa Jeglinski

Melissa Jeglinski
Senior Editor
Silhouette Desire

Please address questions and book requests to:
Silhouette Reader Service
U.S.: 3010 Walden Ave., P.O. Box 1325, Buffalo, NY 14269
Canadian: P.O. Box 609, Fort Erie, Ont. L2A 5X3

Baby at *His* Convenience

KATHIE DeNOSKY

Published by Silhouette Books

America's Publisher of Contemporary Romance

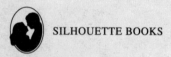 SILHOUETTE BOOKS

ISBN 0-373-76595-9

BABY AT *HIS* CONVENIENCE

Copyright © 2004 by Kathie DeNosky

Visit Silhouette Books at www.eHarlequin.com

Printed in U.S.A.

KATHIE DeNOSKY

lives in her native southern Illinois with her husband and one very spoiled Jack Russell terrier. She writes highly sensual stories with a generous amount of humor. Kathie's books have appeared on the Waldenbooks bestseller list and received the Write Touch Readers' Award from WisRWA and the National Readers' Choice Award. She enjoys going to rodeos, traveling to research settings for her books and listening to country music. Readers may contact Kathie at: P.O. Box 2064, Herrin, Illinois 62948-5264 or e-mail her at kathie@kathiedenosky.com.

To my mother, Margie Ridings,
who loves the Smoky Mountains as much as I do.

And to the memory of
Charles and Barbara Anne Henson. May your legacy
of love and laughter live on in the lives of your children.

One

Dr. Braden's gently worded warning still echoed in Katie Andrews's ears as she stepped out of the Dixie Ridge Clinic into the bright June sunshine.

"With your family history of early menopause, I'm afraid time might be running out for you, Katie. If you intend to have children, it's time to start looking at your options."

At the age of thirty-four, most women weren't faced with the possibility of going through the change of life for at least ten or fifteen years. Unfortunately, Katie wasn't one of them. Every one of her female relatives had started into menopause by the time they were thirty-six. By the time they turned forty, they'd completed the change and their baby-making years were permanently behind them.

Katie bit her lower lip to keep it from trembling. It might already be too late for her to have a child. Her sister Carol Ann and her husband waited until they were in their mid-thirties and had to resort to fertility drugs in order for Carol Ann to become pregnant. The result had been a set of quadruplets.

Katie took a deep, shuddering breath. Although she wanted to have more than one child, she would much rather have them one at a time, instead of all at once. Poor Carol Ann had been so overwhelmed by the demands of taking care of four infants that their parents had left Katie to manage the Blue Bird Café for them, and moved out to California to help their stressed out oldest daughter.

Glancing at her watch, she stuffed the brochure Dr. Braden had given her into her shoulder bag. She'd have to put her baby-making crisis on hold until she closed the café this afternoon.

Right now, she was needed back at the Blue Bird. And if she didn't get there before the lunch rush, Helen McKinney would probably quit on the spot and Katie's parents would never forgive her for losing the best short-order cook in all of eastern Tennessee.

A distant rumble from down the road grew louder and just as she was about to cross the road, a big, shiny red-and-black Harley Davidson roared into a parking space in front of the Blue Bird. The man riding the powerful machine nodded when Katie hurried passed him on the way to the café's entrance, but she couldn't say he actually looked her way as he turned off the motorcycle and removed his mirrored sunglasses.

That wasn't unusual. Since riding into town two months ago, Jeremiah Gunn hadn't become friendly with anyone but Harv Jenkins. In fact, all that anyone seemed to know about him was that he'd moved into Granny Applegate's old place up on Piney Knob and came down every day to eat lunch and talk fly-fishing with Harv. Otherwise, the big man kept to himself. And if his body language was any indication, he wanted it to stay that way.

But to her surprise, when she started to open the café door, a long muscular arm reached around her to take hold of the handle. Glancing over her shoulder, she swallowed hard. It was the first time she'd stood this close to the mysterious Mr. Gunn and she was shocked to find that she had to look up to meet his chocolate-brown gaze. At a fraction of an inch shorter than six feet tall herself, that didn't happen often.

His chest barely brushing her shoulders as he pulled the door open, caused her skin to tingle. ''Th-thank you, Mr. Gunn,'' she stammered, unsure of why she suddenly felt so rattled.

''The name's Jeremiah.'' There was no trace of emotion in his deep baritone, but the sound of it made her heart skip a beat.

Hurrying into the café, Katie put distance between them. Something about being close to the man made her knees weak and had her wondering if she'd lost her mind.

"It's about time you showed up," Helen McKinney called through the open window behind the lunch counter. "I'm already covered up with orders."

"I'm sorry," Katie apologized. She shoved her purse beneath the counter and reached for an apron hanging on a peg beside the cash register. "Doc was running a little late with his morning appointments."

Helen's irritated expression instantly turned to one of concern. "Are you all right?"

Katie nodded. "It was just my annual physical and other than being about fifty pounds heavier than I should be, I'm as healthy as a horse."

Helen shook her head as she ladled white gravy over a mound of mashed potatoes and country-fried steak. "I don't pay any attention to those height and weight charts. I don't know who makes those things up or where they live, but it for darned sure isn't in the real world. I'd look like an understuffed scarecrow if I weighed what the danged things say is right for my height." She pushed the plate through the window for Katie to serve. "This goes to Harv." She reached for another plate. "Don't worry about the others. I've got everyone's order except for Silent Sam over there, talkin' fly-fishin' with Harv."

Nodding, Katie placed Harv's food on the serving

tray, then grabbed an order pad and pencil. "Jeremiah usually asks for the day's special."

"Jeremiah?" Helen cocked an eyebrow and stopped spooning green beans onto a plate to stare at Katie. "Did I miss somethin'? When did you get to be so friendly with him?"

"I'm not," Katie insisted, careful to keep her voice low. "But he's been coming here nearly every day for the past two months. It just doesn't seem right to keep calling him Silent Sam."

"Why Katie Andrews, if I didn't know better, I'd say you were sweet on him," Helen said, her hazel eyes twinkling merrily.

"Oh good heavens, Helen," Katie said impatiently. Why did she suddenly feel so uncharacteristically flustered? "I'm too old to have a crush on anyone."

Grinning, Helen whispered, "You're a woman and you're still breathin' ain't you?" Before Katie could respond, she added, "Shoot, if I wasn't married to Jim, I might even be tempted to set my sights on that one. As my daughter and her friends always say, he's hotter than a firecracker on the Fourth of July."

Katie gave her friend a wan smile. "We don't have time for this, Helen. We have a café full of people waiting for their food."

"Hittin' a little too close to home for you, Katie?" Helen asked, laughing.

"You're not even in the same ball park." Turning,

Katie started around the counter to serve Harv his fried steak. "Now, get back to work, Helen."

Katie cringed as Helen's delighted cackle followed her across the café. The woman wasn't buying her disinterest in Jeremiah Gunn for a minute. But what disturbed her more than anything was the fact that she was having a hard time believing it herself.

Harv Jenkins droned on about the advantages of fly-fishing the smaller streams over one of the larger tributaries like Piney River, but Jeremiah wasn't listening to a word the old guy said. He was too busy wondering what the hell had gotten into him.

For the past two months, he'd ridden his Harley down the mountain each weekday at noon to have lunch in the Blue Bird Café. And every day the waitress everyone called Katie had taken his order.

But today, when he held the door for her to enter the café, it was as if he'd seen her for the first time. Watching her move around behind the counter as she talked to the cook and prepared to serve someone's food, he had to admit that she was a damn fine-looking woman.

But why hadn't he noticed that before? How could he have missed how pretty her aquamarine eyes were or that her long, dark brown hair looked like strands of shiny chestnut-colored silk?

"Did you hear what I just said, boy?" Harv asked, sounding impatient. "Piney River is good for cat fishin', but if I'm wantin' to do some serious trout fishin', I like streams like that one behind your cabin.''

''It's not my cabin,'' Jeremiah answered, turning his attention back to the older gentleman sitting across the worn Formica table from him. ''I'm just renting it for a few months.''

Harv grinned. ''You know, Ray Applegate's been lookin' to sell his grandma's old place.''

Jeremiah figured he knew where the conversation was headed. ''That's what Ray told me when I rented it from him.''

''You decided how long you're gonna stay here on Piney Knob?'' Harv asked.

Harv had been asking that question for the past month. And just as he had each time Harv asked, Jeremiah shook his head and gave him the same answer. ''Nope. I'm just taking it one day at a time and getting used to my new status as a civilian.''

''How long was it you said you were in the Marine Corps?'' Harv asked.

''Nineteen years.''

Jeremiah still felt a keen sense of regret that his military career had come to a premature end. If he hadn't ended up with a bum knee after being injured in that mission a few months ago, he'd still be barking orders to his men and wouldn't be faced with having to decide what he wanted to do with the rest of his life.

"Here you go, Harv," Katie said, setting down a plate of country fried-steak and mashed potatoes covered in enough white gravy to clog every artery in Harv's entire body. Turning her attention to Jeremiah, she smiled. "What can I get for you today…Jeremiah?"

Feeling as if he'd been punched right square in the gut, Jeremiah swallowed hard. She had one of the prettiest smiles he'd ever seen, and the sound of her soft voice saying his name caused a warm feeling to spread throughout his chest.

Clearing his suddenly dry throat, he finally managed to push words past his paralyzed lips. "I'll have whatever the special is for the day."

"One plate of chicken and dumplings, green beans and sliced tomatoes coming right up," she said, jotting his order on the pad of paper in her hand. "And what would you like to drink with that?"

"Iced tea." He didn't bother telling her he wanted the sweetened tea. In Dixie Ridge they didn't serve it any other way.

"Your order will be ready in just a few minutes." She tucked the pad of paper in the front pocket of her apron. "And I'll be right back with your tea."

When she turned to walk over to the lunch counter, Jeremiah noticed the two men sitting at the next table were about to get up. But before he could warn Katie to watch out, the guy closest to her shoved his chair backward and right into her. She staggered and Jeremiah instinctively reached to keep her from falling. Before he knew quite how it happened, he found Katie sitting on his lap.

They stared at each other for endless seconds as several things about her began to register in his startled brain. Katie smelled like peaches and sunshine, and her perfectly shaped lips were parted as if begging for his kiss. But those weren't the only things he noticed. Her body was soft in the way only a woman's could be, and her lush curves pressing against him were causing certain parts of his anatomy to respond in a very male way.

"Sorry about that, Katie," the man who had bumped into her apologized, breaking the spell. "I was braggin' about my new baby girl and wasn't payin' attention to what I was doin'."

"It's all right, Jeff," Katie said, sounding breathless. "How are Freddie and the baby doing?"

"Just fine." Offering his hand to help her to her feet, the man laughed. "But Nick isn't sure he's going to like being a big brother."

Jeremiah wasn't sure why, but when Katie started to accept the man's help, he tightened his arm around her waist, effectively holding her in place. If the startled look she gave him was any indication, she was as surprised by his action as he was.

Glaring at the man she'd called Jeff, Jeremiah watched the guy raise an eyebrow, then wisely move on toward the check-out counter. "Are you sure you're all right?"

Her cheeks colored a pretty pink. "The question is, are *you* all right?"

"Of course." He frowned. "Why wouldn't I be?"

"I sat down pretty hard and…I'm not exactly a lightweight." The blush on her pretty face deepened. Before he could respond, she wiggled out of his grasp, stood up and looked around as if trying to find an escape. "I need to…ring up Jeff's lunch ticket."

Jeremiah stared after her when she hurried toward the cash register sitting at one end of the counter. The gentle sway of her rounded hips as she walked across the café caused his body to tighten further, and he had to force himself to look away.

"Katie's a right pretty girl, ain't she?" Harv asked with a knowing smile.

"I hadn't noticed," Jeremiah lied, trying to sound indifferent. He failed miserably. He knew it and so did Harv.

Suddenly feeling the need to run like hell, Jeremiah stood up and reached for his wallet. "I'm not very hungry today, Harv. I think I'm going to skip lunch and try my luck in the stream behind the cabin. Maybe I'll catch a couple of rainbow trout for supper." Removing a couple of bills, he tossed the money on the table. "This is for the waitress's trouble. When she comes back to bring my tea, tell her to cancel my order."

"Her name's Katie Andrews," Harv said, his wrinkled face splitting into a wide grin. "And in case anybody cares to know, she's single."

Refusing to comment, Jeremiah took his sunglasses out of the pocket of his T-shirt and put them on. "I'll see you tomorrow, Harv."

He purposely avoided looking at Katie as he wove his way through the tables and walked to the door. Once he was outside, he settled himself on the leather seat of his motorcycle and finally released his pent-up breath.

What the hell had gotten into him? Why did he suddenly have the irresistible urge to watch every move Katie Andrews made?

She for damned sure wasn't the kind of woman he normally preferred. He liked his women brazenly sexy, shamelessly uninhibited in the bedroom and as commitment-shy as he was. It kept things simple and uncomplicated that way.

But Katie wasn't the kind of woman that a man loved, then left without a backward glance. Hell, everything about her shouted stability and permanence—the very things he'd spent his entire adult life trying to avoid. So why did he find her so damned fascinating?

He shook his head. He wasn't sure, but what he needed right now was to put as much distance between himself and Katie Andrews as possible.

Starting his Harley, he backed it out of the parking space, then pulled onto the road that led up the side of Piney Knob Mountain. He needed the quiet solitude of his rented cabin, where life was simple and he wouldn't be reminded of all the things that he didn't want and knew damned well he'd never have.

Frowning, Katie tucked the twenty dollars Jeremiah had left on the table into the pocket of her apron. She'd have to see that he got the money back the next time he came in for lunch.

Walking to the window behind the counter, she picked up the piece of paper with his order on it and tore it in half. "Helen, don't bother making up that plate of chicken and dumplings for Jeremiah. He's changed his mind and won't be eating with us today."

"He won't?" Helen looked dumbfounded. "That's the first time Silent Sam has missed eatin' lunch here since he rolled into town."

"His name is Jeremiah," Katie said as she turned her attention back to her duties.

The woman gave her a grin that set Katie's teeth on edge. "That's what you keep tellin' me."

Doing her best to ignore her friend's teasing, Katie started another pot of coffee and tidied up behind the counter. Until today, she hadn't paid much attention to the man who'd cruised into town a little over two months ago on his shiny motorcycle. But in the past half hour her thoughts seemed to have been consumed with him.

From the day he'd first strolled into the café, she'd noticed how ruggedly handsome he was, and how his voice was sexy enough to turn a chunk of granite into a puddle of gravy. A woman would have to be comatose not to notice those things about him.

But she hadn't realized how physically well-built he was, or how his biceps strained the knit fabric of the T-shirts he always wore. When he'd caught her to keep her from falling, she'd been struck speechless at the feel of his rock-hard muscles holding her so securely to his solid frame.

Her cheeks heated at how she'd just sat there on his lap staring at him like a complete ninny. But she'd been thoroughly mesmerized by what she'd seen in his dark brown gaze. Jeremiah Gunn was intelligent, compassionate and, if paying for a meal he'd ordered but didn't eat was any indication, extremely honest.

"All the things I'd like to pass on to my child," she murmured thoughtfully.

Katie caught her breath and quickly looked around to see if anyone had heard her, or noticed the heat she felt coloring her cheeks. Why on earth had the thought even entered her mind? Was she so desperate to have a baby that she'd started looking at complete strangers as father material?

She shook her head. There would be plenty of time after she closed the café to consider her options. Not that Jeremiah Gunn was, or ever would be one of them.

But two hours later, as she stepped out of the Blue Bird and locked the door behind her, she couldn't seem to get the big man off her mind. He had everything she could want for her child—intelligence, a well-proportioned body and good looks.

"Forget it," she muttered to herself as she pulled the colorful pamphlet Dr. Braden had given her out of her shoulder bag. Surely she could find someone at the Lancaster Sperm Bank down in Chattanooga with the same attributes.

As she continued to gaze at the little booklet, she frowned. She wasn't sure that choosing her baby's father from a list of donors in a database was something she wanted to do. She suspected it would feel a lot like she was making a purchase from a mail-order catalog when it came time to select the donor based on a list of their physical characteristics and personality traits.

Lost in thought, she stuffed the booklet back into her bag and started walking down the side of the tree-lined road toward the house she'd lived in all of her life. She barely noticed how the early June sunshine filtered through the leaves, or how the flame azaleas, rhododendrons and mountain laurel added splashes of orange, hot pink and white to the lush green foliage on the side of Piney Knob Mountain. Nor did she pay attention to an occasional car honking a greeting as it drove by. And she wasn't the least bit worried about being run down.

Most of the time, a person could walk down the center of the road from one end of town to the other and never encounter a vehicle from either direction. And as far as she was concerned, it was testament to the fact that Dixie Ridge, Tennessee, was far too small to consider asking any of its male residents to help her with her problem.

Katie sighed. Most of the men she knew were married anyway, and the few who were still single already had fiancées or girlfriends. She couldn't ask any of them to help her have a baby. Somehow, she had a feeling the women in their lives would have a real problem with that.

A feeling of resignation began to fill her. At this point, it looked like the sperm bank was her only choice. It wasn't like eligible prospects were growing on trees around Dixie Ridge. Other than Jeremiah, Homer Parsons was about the only other bachelor in town. And he was ninety years old and had been claimed by Miss Millie Rogers over sixty years ago.

And even though Jeremiah Gunn had every trait she wanted for her child, she would never in a million years be able to work up the courage to ask him to help her. What would she say?

"Mr. Gunn, here's your lunch. And by the way, would you mind stopping by the Dixie Ridge Clinic this afternoon, look at a magazine or watch a video, and make a donation in a plastic cup in order for me to have a baby?"

As she unlocked the back door and let herself into the house, her cheeks felt as if they were on fire. He'd think she was completely insane.

Two

"Harv, what do you say we call it a day?" Jeremiah called as he wound in his line. "It looks like they've stopped biting and by the time I fillet these trout, it'll be time to fry them for supper."

As soon as he'd returned from the diner, Jeremiah had pulled on his waders, grabbed his fly rod and trudged out into the middle of the stream behind his rented cabin. He'd wanted to catch a few trout, and hopefully figure out why he suddenly couldn't put the Blue Bird Café's waitress out of his mind. Unfortunately, his introspection had been cut short when Harv—after finishing his lunch—had driven up Piney Knob to Jeremiah's cabin, waded out into the stream and started chattering like a damn magpie. The older man had covered everything in his ramblings from the differences between fishing lures and flies, to asking Jeremiah's opinion on whether or not Harv should take on a partner in his fishing and hunting business, Piney Knob Outfitters.

Jeremiah had ended up tuning out most of it, but apparently the fish hadn't. Since Harv showed up and started in with his motormouth, Jeremiah hadn't had so much as a nibble.

"What did you catch for your supper? Rainbow or brown trout?" Harv asked, turning to slowly wade back to the stream's rocky bank.

Jeremiah checked the willow basket creel slung over his shoulder. "Four rainbows."

"That oughtta be enough for the two of you," Harv said, over his shoulder.

"The two of us?" Jeremiah frowned. "What the hell are you talking about, Harv?"

"Looks like you're gonna have company for supper." The older man grinned as he raised his hand to wave to someone on the bank. "Afternoon, Katie."

Jeremiah turned so fast he came close to having the fast-moving water knock his feet out from under him. Sure enough, there stood Katie Andrews on the path leading back to the cabin.

"I wonder what she wants?" he asked, thankful his question had been drowned out by the babbling sound of water rushing over the rocks in the stream bed.

Since moving to the Smoky Mountains a couple of months ago, Jeremiah hadn't gone out of his way to get to know any of the Dixie Ridge residents, except for the man trudging through the water ahead of him. And it was impossible not to get acquainted with Harv. The man never shut up. He'd completely ignored Jeremiah's attempts to keep to himself, and before he knew how it happened, he and Harv had become friends—something Jeremiah rarely allowed to happen with anyone.

When they carefully picked their way over the rocks scattered along the stream bank, Jeremiah cursed himself for standing there in front of Katie as speechless as a pimple-faced kid in the presence of the prom queen. Never in all of his thirty-seven years had he ever had a problem talking to women. But for some reason, he couldn't think of a thing to say, nor could he figure out why.

"What brings you up here to the crick, Katie?" Harv asked as he took his fishing rod apart and put the sections in a storage case. "Thinkin' about catchin' yourself a rainbow for supper."

Smiling, she shook her head. "Not today, Harv."

"Do you fish?" Jeremiah asked, finally getting his tongue to work.

"I've been known to catch a fish now and then," she said, nodding.

Harv's laughter indicated there was more to her fishing experience than she was letting on. "Katie's won the Fourth of July Powder-Puff Fishin' Derby for the past eight years. And she was runner-up for four or five years before that." Chuckling, he finished storing his fishing rod and snapped the case shut. "I 'spect she's a shoo-in for this year's title, too."

"Is that so?" Jeremiah didn't doubt that a woman could be good at the sport of fly-fishing. He'd just never met one before.

She shrugged one shoulder. "My dad and brother started taking me fishing with them when I was four years old."

They stood, staring at each other for several strained moments before Harv finally asked, "If you didn't come up this way to go fishin', what did you come up here for, Katie?"

Jeremiah watched a rosy blush color her porcelain cheeks. Good Lord, he couldn't remember the last time he'd seen a woman blush.

"I…um, came to talk to Mr. Gunn about the money he left at the café," she said, sounding uncertain.

"Didn't I tell you she wasn't none to happy about you leavin' that twenty bucks?" Harv asked, starting down the path to the cabin.

"Yeah, Harv, you told me," Jeremiah muttered, waiting for Katie to fall into step ahead of him.

Actually, Harv had reiterated that fact at least a

dozen times over the course of the past two hours, and each time he told the story Katie was a little more angry than the time before. By the time Harv got finished embellishing the actual facts, it had sounded as if she was ready to tear him apart with her bare hands for leaving the money.

As they walked the short distance to the house, Jeremiah tried not to notice how her well-worn jeans hugged her long legs, or the sensual sway of her full hips. By the time they reached the cabin, sweat beaded his forehead and his own jeans felt as if they'd shrunk a couple of sizes in the stride.

What had gotten into him? He wasn't some oversexed teenager with nothing but hormones racing through his veins. He was a grown man and should have gained a little more control over the years than that. Had he been so long without a woman's charms that just watching one walk in front of him turned him on?

"Well, I'm gonna leave you two kids to fight it out over that money," Harv said, heading toward his truck. He tossed his fishing rod case into the back. "Sadie'll take a strip off my hide a mile wide if I don't get home in time for supper."

"Tell her I said hello." Katie waved as the older man opened the driver's door and slid behind the wheel. "And I'll see you tomorrow at the Blue Bird, Harv."

Once Harv's truck disappeared down the lane, Jeremiah tried to think of something to say. When nothing came to mind, he motioned toward the cabin's front porch. "Would you like to sit down?"

She looked uncertain, then taking a deep breath, nodded and preceded him up the steps. Before she sat down on the wooden porch swing, she pulled two ten dollar bills from the front pocket of her jeans.

"Here's your money," she said, handing the money to him.

He shook his head as he seated himself on the bench facing the swing. "I left that to pay for the lunch I ordered and a tip for your trouble."

She stuffed the money into his hand. "Canceling the order was no big deal. And that was too much for a tip anyway."

An electric current zinged up his arm when her fingers touched the palm of his hand and he had to swallow hard to keep from groaning. "But—"

She shook her head as she lowered herself onto the swing. "I didn't do anything to earn it."

He admired her principles, but he wished like hell she'd kept the money and left him alone. For some reason that he couldn't quite figure out, Katie Andrews made him about as edgy as a raw recruit doing a belly crawl through a swamp full of alligators.

"Mr. Gunn, there's something—"

"Jeremiah," he interrupted. Needing something to do to keep from staring at her, he pulled the little table he used to make fishing flies closer. "The name's Jeremiah."

"Oh, yes. Sorry. I forgot." She sounded a little breathless and a quick glance her way told him she had more on her mind than returning his twenty bucks. "There's something I'd like to discuss with you, Jeremiah."

He picked up the fly he'd been working on that morning and began to wrap red nylon thread around the tiny feathers hiding the fishhook. He couldn't imagine what she wanted to talk to him about, but he could tell that whatever it was made her nervous as hell.

"I'm listening."

She stood up and began to pace the length of the porch. "This isn't easy for me. I've never done anything like this before."

He glanced up in time to see her nibbling on her lower lip as if she was trying to work up her courage. "Whatever it is, it can't be *that* bad," he said, trying not to think how cute she looked. "Why don't you just say what you have to say and get it over with?"

She stared at him for several seconds before she gave a short nod. "All right, Mr. Gunn—I mean Jeremiah." He watched her close her eyes and take a deep breath before opening them to meet his gaze head-on. "Would you be willing to consider helping me have a baby?"

Jeremiah had no idea what he'd expected her to

say, but asking him to help her procreate wasn't it. More shocked by her request than he'd ever been by anything in his life, he forgot all about watching what he was doing and suddenly felt a sharp jab as the fishhook sank deep into the fleshy pad of his thumb. "Son of a bit—"

"Oh dear heavens!" Katie rushed over to take his hand in hers. "I'm so sorry," she said, examining the injury. "I didn't mean to startle you."

As painful as it was to have a fishhook piercing his thumb, her soft hands holding his overrode the discomfort. All he could think about was the fact that she was standing close enough that if he raised his head their lips would touch. He suddenly felt hot all over and his heart rate increased considerably.

"It'll be all right once I get the hook out," he said, trying to pull away from her. He needed to put some distance between them before he did something stupid like grab her and kiss her until they both went limp from lack of oxygen.

"The barb is in too deep," she said, releasing his hand. "Dr. Braden is going to have to deal with this."

"I can take care of it."

"No, you can't," she insisted. The concern in her expressive gaze caused a warm feeling to spread throughout his chest. "Have you had a tetanus shot recently?"

He nodded. If he'd been able to get his vocal cords to work, he would have told her that the marines made sure their men were always current on their immunizations. But at the moment, he couldn't have strung a sentence together if his life depended on it.

"Come on," she said, tugging on his arm. "I'll drive you down to the clinic."

"That's not necessary," he said, even as he rose to his feet. "I can drive myself."

"Do you have a car or truck?"

He shook his head. "No. All I have is my Harley."

She gave him a look that clearly stated she thought he was being a stubborn fool. "Don't you think it would be a little difficult holding on to it without driving the fishhook even farther into your thumb?"

Frowning, Jeremiah looked at the tarp covering his Harley parked a few feet from the porch. He hadn't thought about how he'd manage to use the handle grip gas feed.

"That's what I thought. You can't." She pointed toward her red SUV. "I'll take you to the clinic."

"But I can take a pair of pliers and—"

"Make matters worse," she interrupted. "Now get in my truck." Without another word, she started down the steps toward her Explorer.

As Jeremiah followed Katie to the SUV, he had to admit she would have made a good marine. She hadn't gotten squeamish the way some women might have done when she looked at the hook protruding from his thumb, nor had she passed out when she saw the blood seeping out around it. She'd kept her head, assessed what needed to be done, then prepared to execute her plan of action—much like any good soldier would do.

Sliding into the passenger side of the truck, he glanced over at her. But even as he admired her take-charge attitude, he wasn't so sure she might not be a little touched in the head.

What in the name of hell had prompted her to ask him to help her make a baby?

As Katie held the door open for Jeremiah to enter the Dixie Ridge Clinic, she wished for at least the hundredth time that the ground would open up and swallow her. What on earth had she been thinking when she asked if he'd be willing to consider helping her have a child?

After she'd gone home, she'd decided to drive up Piney Knob to return his money and to ask him a few leading questions that might help her gauge his receptiveness to being the sperm donor for her baby. She'd had absolutely no intention of actually asking him to be the father.

But instead of handling the situation with diplomacy and tact, she'd thrown out her request like a hand grenade. And he'd recoiled as if the darned thing had been a real bomb and not a metaphorical one. If his reaction was any indication, he not only wouldn't be willing to help her have a child, he'd probably never speak to her again.

"Hey there, Katie," Martha Payne called from the reception counter. She eyed Jeremiah up and down. "Looks like you found someone—"

"With a fishhook in his thumb," Katie interrupted her. "He needs Doc to remove it."

Martha had been the nurse at the Dixie Ridge Clinic since forever and knew everything that went on within its walls. She no doubt thought Katie had found a hapless victim to make a donation toward Operation: Katie-Wants-a-Baby-Before-It's-Too-Late.

"Good thing you got here when you did," Martha said, patting a few strands of steel-gray hair back into place as she came around the end of the counter to take a look at Jeremiah's thumb. "As soon as we close up for the day, Doc and Lexi are gonna load up their three kids and take off for a couple days vacation down at Stone Mountain in Georgia." She shook her head as she examined the wound. "You buried that hook real good, son. How did it happen?"

Katie's face grew hot when Jeremiah glanced over at her. "I was tying a fly and wasn't paying attention to what I was doing," he said, shrugging. "It happens."

Martha nodded as she released his hand. "You two have a seat while I get everything set up for Doc to take care of gettin' it out."

As she watched Martha lumber down the hall to one of the examining rooms, Katie sank into one of the chairs lining the walls of the waiting area. She'd seen the gleam in Martha's eyes and knew the woman was dying to know what was going on. Aside from the fact that she wasn't used to seeing Katie with a man, Martha was wondering why Katie had been the one to bring Jeremiah into the clinic. Everyone in town knew that Harv was the only Dixie Ridge resident Jeremiah was acquainted with and would have been the likely candidate to drive him to the clinic.

When Jeremiah settled his tall frame into the chair beside her, she sighed. "This is all my fault and I'm so very sorry."

For the first time since she'd met him, the corners of his mouth curved upward in a rare smile. It changed his whole demeanor.

Her heart skipped a beat and her breath lodged in her lungs. Jeremiah Gunn wasn't just good-looking. When he smiled, he was drop-dead gorgeous.

"Forget about it." He shook his head. "I'm sure I misunderstood what you meant when you said—"

"Well, hello again," Dr. Braden said, smiling as he walked out of his private office. "I didn't expect to see you here again so soon, Katie."

"I'm not here because I need to see you," she said hastily.

Before she could explain things further, Dr. Braden turned his attention to Jeremiah. "So, you're here to see me?"

Jeremiah nodded. "I told Katie I was fine, but she

insisted that you needed to check things over and be the one to take it out.''

Dr. Braden's eyebrows rose as a stunned look spread across his face. ''It really is best for both parties to have a clean bill of health before proceeding with something like this. But you'll be the one to take care of the actual—''

''You mean I have to have a physical, then take this fishhook out myself?'' Jeremiah asked, frowning as he held up his thumb.

Katie's cheeks felt as if they were on fire when Dr. Braden glanced her way. There wasn't a thing she could say that wouldn't make matters worse. All she could do was pray that this nightmare came to an end soon.

Turning his attention back to Jeremiah, Dr. Braden nodded toward the hall. ''I'm afraid I misunderstood the reason for your visit. If you'll follow me, we'll get that hook out and you can be on your way.''

As she watched the two men disappear into the examining room at the far end of the hall, Katie wished with all her heart that this day had never happened. When she'd gotten out of bed this morning, all she'd had on her mind was to get her yearly physical out of the way, work at the café until closing time, then go home and start a new quilt to sell to one of the gift shops in Gatlinburg.

She rubbed her temples with her fingertips. How

had everything gotten so complicated? So humiliating?

Sighing heavily, she leaned back in the chair and closed her eyes. As soon as she drove Jeremiah back up the mountain to the cabin he was renting, she'd make some excuse about temporary insanity running in her family. Then she'd go home and hope with all her heart that she would never have to face him again.

After Dr. Braden had given him a shot in the knuckle to numb his thumb, Jeremiah sat on the examining table and watched the man carefully remove the fishhook from the fleshy part of his thumb. But instead of concentrating on what the doctor was doing, his mind was on the conversation that had taken place in the waiting room.

"You thought I was here for an entirely different reason than having a fishhook taken out of my thumb." It wasn't a question, and if he was any judge of character, Jeremiah knew Dr. Braden wouldn't try to deny it.

The man met Jeremiah's gaze head-on. "Yes."

"I don't guess you're at liberty to tell me what that reason was?" Jeremiah watched Braden cut the barb off the end of the fishhook, then pull the rest of it out of his thumb.

"No, I can't discuss it," Dr. Braden said, applying a generous amount of ointment to the wound. "Let's just say I was wrong in my assumption and leave it at that.''

Jeremiah smiled. ''In other words, if I want to know, Katie's the one who'll have to tell me.''

The doctor grinned as he wrapped gauze around Jeremiah's thumb. ''That's about the size of it.'' He taped the bandage in place, then stepped back for Jeremiah to stand up. ''I'm assuming since you just got out of the military a tetanus shot won't be necessary?''

Jeremiah frowned. He wasn't at all comfortable being the talk of the town. ''Let me guess, Harv told you I was in the marines.''

Braden nodded. ''Don't be too ticked off at old Harv. Having everyone know all about you is one of the hazards of living in a town the size of Dixie Ridge.'' He laughed. ''When I moved here from Chicago five years ago, having everyone know who I was or what I was doing was one of the hardest things for me to get used to. But it didn't take me long to figure out it's their way of letting you know they care about you and want to make you feel like you're part of the community.''

''I'm sure that *was* an adjustment.''

Jeremiah refrained from telling the good doctor there were two sides to every scenario. It had been his experience that small-town gossip was far more destructive and alienating than it had ever been accepting.

As he prepared to leave the treatment room, Dr. Braden pointed to Jeremiah's thumb. "You don't want that to become infected. Let it heal for a few days before you go fishing again."

"Thanks. I'll do that."

Following the man out into the hall, Jeremiah stopped at the reception desk to pay for the doctor's services, then walked into the waiting area where he'd left Katie. As soon as he entered the room, he couldn't help but notice the apprehension in her aquamarine eyes.

"Is everything all right?" she asked, rising to her feet.

He nodded and held up his left hand. "The hook is out and I'm ready to go."

"Good." A sudden clap of thunder caused her to jump. "I need to drive you to the cabin and get back down the mountain before the storm hits."

As they walked across the parking lot to her SUV, Jeremiah frowned at the sight of dark clouds beginning to appear over the top of the mountains west of Dixie Ridge. It had rained almost every day for the past two months. Sometimes it was just a light shower, but other times storms came up from the other side of the mountain and dumped several inches of water in a very short time. It looked as if today it would be the latter.

"Does it rain like this all the time, or is this a

particularly wet year?'' he asked, sliding into the passenger side of the Explorer.

''It's been a pretty normal year,'' she answered as she started the truck and steered it onto the road leading out of Dixie Ridge. ''Here in town we average about fifty inches of rain a year. But up on top of Piney Knob the average is more like sixty inches.''

''That's a lot of rain.''

She nodded. ''A meteorologist could explain it better than I could, but it has something to do with the clouds coming over the mountains.''

''I guess that explains why the creek regularly floods the ford across the road just south of the cabin,'' he said, thinking aloud.

She drove a little faster when fat raindrops began to plop on the hood and windshield of the SUV. ''And that's why I need to get back down the mountain as soon as possible. If I don't, I'll have to wait to cross the creek after the water recedes sometime tomorrow.''

He wasn't entirely comfortable taking the hairpin turns leading up the side of Piney Knob at the rate of speed Katie was driving on the rain-slick roads, but Jeremiah decided it was safer to keep his mouth shut and not distract her. Only after they were on the other side of the creek did he breathe a little easier. The water was higher than its normal ten inches when she eased the truck across the ford, but it hadn't risen to the point where it would flood out the engine when she crossed it on her way back down the mountain.

"Do me a favor," he said when she pulled to a stop in front of the cabin. "Don't drive like a bat out of hell when you go back down the mountain."

Before she could take him to task over his criticism of her driving, he opened the passenger door, got out and sprinted through the increasingly heavy rain to the porch. By the time he climbed the steps and turned back to watch her leave, the taillights of the SUV were already disappearing around the curve of the driveway.

Jeremiah shook his head as he pulled his key from the pocket of his jeans to let himself inside. "Women! She'll probably drive even faster just because I told her to take it easy."

He removed his boots and left them on a mat by the door, then padded over to the fireplace on the opposite side of the great room in his sock feet. Even though it was June and fairly warm, the rain had caused the outside temperature to drop considerably and drenched as he was from his run through the rain, a fire would chase away the chill and feel good by the time the sun set.

As he placed a couple of logs on the grate and put kindling around them, he thought about Katie driving back down the mountain. He didn't like the idea of her navigating the dangerous road in this kind of weather, and he could kick himself for not telling her to call when she got home to let him know she'd arrived safely.

His heart stalled. Now, where had that come from?

Katie was nice enough, but he didn't really know her. And besides, she wasn't his to worry about. Nor did he ever intend for her to be.

He'd spent most of his adult life avoiding her type like the plague. But that didn't mean he couldn't be concerned for her well-being, did it? He'd be just as bothered if it was Harv driving back down the mountain in a driving rain.

Satisfied that he'd discovered the explanation for his uncharacteristic anxiety, he rose to his feet and pulled his wet T-shirt over his head to drop it on the hearth. He'd wait a reasonable period of time, check the phone directory for her number, then call to make sure she'd made it down the mountain without incident. Once he'd done that, he could go about his business with a clear conscience.

Pleased with himself for coming up with a reasonable solution, he unbuckled his belt and popped the snap on his jeans. But just as he started to lower the zipper, something thumped against the old wooden door hard enough to take it off the hinges.

When it happened again, Jeremiah grabbed the shotgun from the gun rack over the fireplace and cautiously approached the door. The sound hadn't been the rhythmic sound of someone knocking, but more an erratic pounding. It was highly possible one of the many black bears in the area had lumbered up onto the porch seeking shelter from the storm.

Pushing the curtain on the back of the door aside, he tried to see what had caused the sound, but nothing seemed out of the ordinary. Convinced that the wind had slammed the swing into the side of the cabin, he turned to put the shotgun back over the fireplace when something thumped against the bottom of the door yet again.

Ready to scare off whatever creature was causing the disturbance, he grabbed the knob, counted to three and threw the door open with a war cry that would have impressed the hell out of any of the superior officers he'd served under. But instead of finding a bear or raccoon on the other side, Jeremiah discovered a wet, mud-covered Katie slumped in a defeated heap at his feet.

Three

_____

When Jeremiah shouted loud enough to wake the dead, Katie would have jumped back and screamed at the top of her lungs if she'd had the energy. As it was, all she could manage was a flinch and a pitiful whimper.

"My God, Katie, what happened?" He propped the gun he held against the door frame, then reached down to pull her to her feet. When her legs threatened to buckle, his strong arms closed around her and he pulled her to his wide, bare chest. "Are you all right, honey?"

She started to answer him, but her teeth were chattering so badly she finally just shook her head and burrowed deeper into the warmth of his big body. She was soaked from the top of her head to the soles of her feet and colder than she'd ever been in her life.

"Come on. Let's go inside by the fire where you can warm up."

Her legs were so stiff they didn't want to work and before she knew what happened, Jeremiah swung her up into his arms and carried her over to set her on the raised hearth of the stone fireplace. She didn't want to think what might be running through his mind about how much she weighed. At the moment she was too preoccupied with whether or not she was going to freeze to death.

"I'll be right back," he said, trotting down the hall. When he returned, he knelt in front of her to drape a thick, fluffy towel around her head and shoulders. He wiped water from her face with another towel, then started to unbutton her blouse.

"N-n-no." Her protest lost most of its effectiveness when her teeth continued to click together like the false sets sold in novelty shops, and her body shook as wave after wave of chills swept over her.

"You're close to being hypothermic," he said, continuing to work at getting the buttons through the soaked fabric. "We have to get you out of these clothes and warmed up, fast. Otherwise, there's a chance you could go into shock."

"I—I'll…b-be f-fine," she said, making her mouth

form the words. She wrapped her cold, stiff fingers around his in an effort to stop him.

"No, you won't be fine," he said firmly.

To her horror, the buttons on her blouse went flying in all directions when he impatiently ripped the wet garment open and peeled it from her body. But her biggest humiliation was yet to come. Reaching behind her, he unhooked her bra and took it off as well.

If she'd thought her day had been bad up to this point, it had just turned into a complete disaster. Goose bumps covered her exposed skin, but Katie wasn't sure if her reaction was due to being colder than she could ever remember, or from having Jeremiah strip her from the waist up. Either way, she was sure that if it was possible for a person to die of embarrassment, she should be expiring at any moment.

Folding her arms over her chest, she covered herself the best she could, while at the same time trying to make herself as small as possible. But that was darned difficult, considering her size.

Her mortification grew with each passing second as he began to vigorously rub her upper arms, shoulders and back with a second plush towel. "One of the first lessons of basic survival is to get out of wet clothes and into something dry," he said as if he was teaching a class on the subject.

She wasn't sure whether to be thankful that he hadn't been affected by the sight of her breasts, or disappointed by the fact that he obviously found her unappealing. But as his ministrations worked their magic and she felt warmth begin to seep back into her chilled body, she decided she didn't care.

"I—I don't feel…as c-cold now." At least her teeth had stopped chattering enough to let her speak.

"Good." He handed her the towel he held, removed her tennis shoes and soggy socks, then stood up. "Take off the rest of your clothes here by the fire, while I get the water running in the shower."

She immediately wrapped the towel around her chest. "The shower?"

He nodded. "A hot shower will help get the blood circulating and bring your temperature back to normal."

As she stared at him, she began to notice several things that she hadn't paid attention to when he first opened the door. Jeremiah Gunn was more than an excellent example of a man in his prime, his body was absolutely beautiful.

His shoulders were impossibly wide, his chest broad, and he had enough ripples on his stomach to make a bodybuilder jealous. A thin coating of black hair covered his impressive pectoral and abdominal muscles, enhancing their definition and perfect tone, while a tattoo of the Marine Corps insignia drew attention to his rock-hard left biceps. A small white scar ran horizontally along the outside of his right upper arm and another marred the tanned skin on his right side.

"I was grazed by a couple of sniper bullets during Desert Storm," he said, apparently noticing her inspection of his body. He shook his head. "But that's ancient history. Right now you need to get out of the rest of those wet clothes."

A shiver that had nothing whatsoever to do with being chilled raced up her spine when the muscles on his right arm flexed as he reached out to help her to her feet. Katie did her best to hold the towel in place over her breasts when she accepted his hand, and forcing her stiff knees to straighten, she rose from the hearth.

"I can start the shower myself," she said firmly. "Where's your bathroom?"

He motioned toward the hall. "First door on the right. While you take a shower, I'll get a pair of sweatpants and a shirt for you to put on."

She gathered as much of her dignity as she could muster and walked in the direction he'd indicated. She'd suffered enough embarrassment for one night, thank you very much. After showing up on his porch looking for all the world like a drowned rat, she'd had her breasts exposed, and been caught staring at him like a hungry dog eyeing a juicy bone. There was no way she was going to add to her humiliation by taking off her jeans and panties until she was safely behind the closed bathroom door.

"When you get the sweats, you can hand them in to me."

Jeremiah followed Katie across the great room. "Make sure the water is good and hot."

When she nodded and shut the door in his face, Jeremiah continued on to his bedroom. His hands shook as he shucked the rest of his own wet clothes and pulled on a set of warm sweats.

Having to remove Katie's shirt and bra had really done a number on his libido. The sight of her full breasts with their coral nipples beaded to pebble hardness from the cold, had almost caused him to have a coronary. The woman had a body that a man could lose himself in, and unless he missed his guess, she didn't even know it.

Most women thought they weren't appealing unless they were thin enough to blow away with the first stiff breeze. He shook his head. A man was never sure when he hugged one of them that he wasn't going to break her in half. No, he liked his women with soft, well-rounded curves just like Katie's.

His body heated and he had to take several deep breaths to calm himself. Thinking about her in those terms wasn't smart. He was a love 'em and leave 'em kind of guy and she was the type of woman a man settled down with and had four or five kids.

Frowning, he pulled another set of gray sweats and a thick pair of socks from the dresser drawer. With everything that had happened in the past few hours, he'd forgotten about what started the chain of events leading up to Katie collapsing on his porch in a muddy heap. Had she really been serious about wanting him to consider helping her make a baby?

Jeremiah thought about what she'd asked just before he'd run the hook into his thumb, and what had taken place at the clinic. He had tried to tell himself that he'd misunderstood what she'd been asking, but in light of Dr. Braden's initial reaction when he saw Jeremiah sitting next to Katie in the waiting room, he was certain he'd heard her right. Hell, how could a man misunderstand a woman asking him point-blank if he would consider helping her have a child?

Walking back down the hall to the bathroom, he decided that as soon as she got dressed, he was going to ask a couple of questions of his own. He fully intended to get to the bottom of the mystery and find out what everyone else seemed to know that he didn't.

Lightly tapping on the door, he listened for a response. The only sound he heard was the shower running full force.

As he opened the door a crack and checked the mirror above the sink, he could see Katie's silhouette through the shower curtain on the opposite side of the bathroom. He'd put the sweats on the counter, then wait for her in the great room.

But his good intentions flew right out the window when movement in the shower drew his attention and stopped him dead in his tracks. Even though it was just a shadowy image through an opaque shower curtain, he could see that Katie's lush breasts thrust upward when she raised her arms to rinse her hair. His mouth went as dry as a sun-bleached bone in the middle of a desert.

He gave himself a mental shake to clear his head, turned and quietly slipped back out into the hall before she noticed him and accused him of being some kind of weirdo. Wondering if he might not be losing it after all, he walked into the kitchen and started a pot of coffee. What was there about Katie Andrews that had him tied in knots? More important, why?

At his age, he'd been around the block more times than he cared to admit and had seen more than a few nude women in his time. But Katie was different. The sight of her body left him speechless and wondering if he'd ever breathe again. And he'd only seen her breasts. What would happen if he was allowed to take off all of her clothes and run his hands over her lush curves, to learn all of her feminine secrets?

"Jeremiah?"

Snapped back to reality by the sound of her soft voice calling his name, he took a deep breath and went back into the great room. He found her sitting on the hearth finger-combing her long, dark hair.

"Warmer now?" he asked, sinking into the chair across from her.

"Yes, thank you."

An uneasy silence stretched between them for several long seconds as he tried to figure out how to broach the baby-making subject. Deciding to wait until an opportunity presented itself, he asked the second question running through his mind.

"What happened after you dropped me off and headed back down the mountain?"

She closed her eyes as her cheeks flushed bright red. "I made it across the creek in the SUV, but I must have punctured a tire on something the rain swept into the ford." Sighing, she shook her head. "I know better than to cross a creek on foot when the water is rising, but I didn't think it had gotten *that* deep."

Jeremiah's heart stalled. "You waded back across the damned thing?"

"Yes." Nibbling on her lower lip, her blush deepened. "By the time I got out and checked the tire, the water had risen to above my knees and was faster than I anticipated. When I got to the middle of the ford the current knocked my feet out from under me and I ended up facedown in about three feet of water."

The thought of what might have happened caused a tight knot to form in his stomach. If she'd been swept downstream there was a good chance she'd have gone over the waterfall and plunged sixty feet into the gorge below.

"Dammit, Katie." He sat forward. "Aside from the fact that the water temperature is ice-cold, you could have drowned or—"

"Gone over Piney Falls." She scrunched her eyes

shut for a moment. "I thought of that while I was floundering around trying to find something to hang on to so that I could get my feet back under me."

She looked so vulnerable sitting there in his oversized gray sweats it was all he could do to keep from taking her into his arms. Suddenly needing distance between them, he got up and walked toward the kitchen.

"Would you like a cup of coffee?"

"That would be nice. Thank you."

At the door, he turned to ask, "Sugar or cream?"

"A little of both, please."

"How about something to eat? I think I've got some cold cuts and cheese. I could make a sandwich for you."

"Thanks, but I'm not very hungry." Her tentative smile did strange things to his insides and had him wondering if she tasted as sweet as she looked.

Deciding retreat was the better part of valor, he walked over to the kitchen counter, propped his hands on the edge and took several deep breaths. He had to get a grip and figure out what there was about Katie that made him want to take her into his arms and kiss her senseless.

As he poured their coffee, he decided it had to be his lack of female companionship for the past year. He hadn't been with a woman since just before he was sent to the Middle East. That had been a little over twelve months ago and it was only natural that a man would suffer a few effects from being celibate that long.

Relieved that he'd found the explanation for his uncharacteristic edginess, he returned to the great room with two mugs of coffee. "All I had was the powdered creamer. Hope that's all right."

"That's fine." She took the cup from him, but didn't look up.

"It turned out all right, Katie," he said, figuring the events of the evening were catching up with her. "You're safe now."

"I know." When she finally glanced up at him there was a fine sheen of moisture filling her pretty eyes. "Have you ever had a day you wished had never happened?"

"I think we've all had days like that, honey." It was becoming increasingly more difficult to keep from pulling her to him.

"Yes, but this has been the worst day of my life," she said, sounding miserable.

Sitting down beside her on the hearth, he rested his forearms on his knees and held his coffee mug between them with both hands. "Why do you say that?"

"I've done nothing but make a fool of myself this entire day." She pointed to his hand. "Does your thumb hurt?"

He shook his head. "This is nothing compared to being shot by a sniper."

They both fell silent, and knowing this was the opening he'd waited for, Jeremiah asked, "Why did you ask me about helping you have a baby, Katie?"

Once he'd thrown the question out, he wished he'd used a little more tact, or at least eased into the subject. He felt like a total jerk when she recoiled as if she'd been struck.

"You must have misunderstood," she said defensively. "I didn't mean—"

"Then why did Dr. Braden think I was at the clinic to get a clean bill of health and make a donation?"

She slowly set her cup on the hearth, then clasped her hands into a white-knuckled knot in her lap. "I'd really appreciate you forgetting about that," she said, her voice little more than a whisper.

Jeremiah put down his own mug, then reached over to take her hands in his. "That's going to be hard to do, Katie. It's not every day that a woman asks me to help her make a baby."

Pulling away from him, she stood up and walked over to the picture window. "It's not…that easy to explain."

He gave her the space she obviously needed and remained seated by the fireplace. He could tell the reason behind her request was extremely personal. But she'd brought him into this when she'd asked for his help. And that was something *he* took pretty damned personal.

"Why don't you start at the beginning?"

She took a deep breath and squared her shoulders as she looked out at the approaching darkness. "I had an appointment for my annual physical this morning. I found out that time is running out for me."

His heart sped up. Did she have major health problems?

"And?" he prompted when she fell silent.

She turned to face him. "Dr. Braden told me that if I intend to have children, I'd better do it now because in a couple of years there's a good chance that I won't be able to conceive."

Jeremiah frowned. "I know women are always concerned about their biological clocks, but that shouldn't be an issue for several more years."

"But it is." Looking defeated, she walked back to the hearth to sit down. "The female members of my family have a history of early menopause. Most of them start into the change around the age of thirty-six and by the time they reach forty they're no longer fertile." She paused to meet his gaze head-on. "I turned thirty-four last week."

Digesting what she'd said, he frowned. "I can see why that would present a problem. But isn't there someone in town you'd rather—"

"Dixie Ridge is so small there aren't that many

single men to begin with,'' she said, cutting him off. ''And the majority of them aren't suitable.''

''Why not?''

''They're either over the age of eighty, or haven't made it out of kindergarten yet.'' She shrugged one shoulder. ''The handful that's left are either engaged or seeing someone.'' She gave him a pointed look. ''I imagine their fiancées or girlfriends would take a dim view of my asking them to be the donor for my baby.''

''What about going to a sperm bank?'' he asked, wondering why she hadn't explored that route to begin with.

''That's not an option for me,'' she replied, her tone leaving no doubt that she meant what she said. ''I'd feel like I was placing an order through a mail-order catalog. Besides, I want to know the donor. I don't want to read about the traits he'll be passing on to my baby. I want to see them.''

Curiosity got the better of him. ''And you think I have what you're looking for?''

Nodding, she didn't hesitate when she recited his characteristics. ''You're tall, in good physical condition, obviously healthy, and reasonably good-looking.'' Taking a breath, she finished. ''You're also brave, intelligent and honest.''

''What makes you think I'm intelligent and honest?'' he asked, fascinated by her assessment of him.

''I've heard Harv telling people that you were a

highly decorated sergeant major in the marines and had led your squad on several missions in the Middle East." She smiled. "You couldn't be a coward or dull-witted to do that."

Despite wanting to throttle Harv for being a gossip, Jeremiah couldn't help but laugh. "I know a few privates and a couple of corporals who would argue that last point with you, honey."

She shrugged. "Facts are facts. You brought the men in your squad back from the missions alive, didn't you?"

"It was my job," he said nodding. "But that doesn't explain why you think I'm honest."

"You could have walked out of the Blue Bird today without attempting to pay for your meal." She stopped to hide a yawn behind her delicate hand, then shaking her head, she smiled. "But you left the money with Harv, along with word to cancel your order. A dishonest person would have just walked out and left us with a plate of food to throw away."

The look of unwavering confidence in her blue-green gaze robbed him of breath. To say it unnerved him was an understatement.

Needing time to put things in perspective and come up with a plausible excuse why he wouldn't be a suitable donor for her child, Jeremiah stood up and checked his watch. "It's after nine and you've already been yawning. What do you say we turn in for the night?'' He pointed toward the hall. ''You can have my room and I'll bed down here on the couch.''

''I can't take your bed,'' she said, rising from her seat on the hearth. ''I've already caused you enough trouble. I'll sleep out here.''

''I insist,'' he said, placing his hands on her shoulders to turn her toward the hall.

The feel of her warmth through his heavy sweatshirt, and the complete faith in him shining in her pretty eyes, sent his temperature skyward and had his heart thumping against his ribs so hard he wasn't sure she couldn't hear it. She didn't even know him, yet she believed in his integrity—trusted that he was as honorable as old Harv had led her to believe. Jeremiah had never had anyone outside of the military display that kind of confidence in him.

Before he could stop himself, he pulled her to him and brushed his mouth over hers. ''Although I sympathize with your predicament, I'm not the man you're looking for, Katie.''

When her perfect lips parted on a soft sigh, Jeremiah gave in to the temptation that had been gnawing at him since she landed on his lap at the Blue Bird. Slipping his tongue inside, he explored her inner recesses and acquainted himself with the taste of her. She was even sweeter than he'd imagined and her shy response to his probing sent his blood pressure skyward.

She lifted her arms to his shoulders as if she needed

support and Jeremiah didn't think twice about pressing her against him. Very few women were tall enough for him to feel their feminine softness pressed from his chest to his knees, but Katie's body fit his perfectly. His lower body hardened so fast it left him feeling light-headed, and there was no doubt in his mind that she felt his insistent arousal when she went completely still, then tried to pull away from him.

Slowly breaking the kiss, he continued to hold her as he whispered close to her ear. "I want you to go into the bedroom now, Katie." He kissed the satiny skin along the column of her neck down to her shoulder. "Otherwise, I just might forget that I'm supposed to be a trustworthy gentleman."

When he released her and stepped back, he silently cursed himself for being so damned honorable. Her lips were moist and slightly swollen from his kiss and her creamy skin wore the blush of unfulfilled desire. He'd never seen a woman look more beautiful than Katie did at that very moment.

"Jeremiah, I—"

"Don't tempt a man when he's doing his damnedest to do the right thing, Katie." Taking another step back, he nodded toward the hall. "Now go to bed."

He noticed the confusion in her blue-green gaze and had to fight the urge to take her back into his arms. But to his relief, she turned and quickly walked down the hall to his room.

Only after he heard the bedroom door close did

Jeremiah draw another breath. It had taken everything
he had to let her go, when what he really wanted to
do was join Katie in his bed and spend the rest of the
night losing himself in her soft body.

And that scared the living hell out of him.

Walking back to the overstuffed armchair on legs
that threatened to fold, he sank down on the plush
cushion, and rubbing his bad knee, stared into the
flames of the rapidly dying fire. Why did he find Katie
so damned sexy?

She didn't flirt with shameless confidence like most
of the women he'd been attracted to. Hell, Katie
wasn't even aware of the effect she had on a man.
And if her innocent response to his kiss was anything
to go by, he'd bet everything he owned that she was
far from uninhibited in the bedroom.

So why did he find her so damned irresistible?

He ran a shaky hand through his thick hair. Katie
was his opposite in so many ways it was ridiculous.
She'd always had stability in her life, while he'd been
bounced from one foster home to another after being
abandoned at the age of five by his unwed mother.
Katie came from a close-knit community of family
and friends. The only family he could claim, and the
only place where he ever felt that he'd belonged, had
been in the Marine Corps. And he'd lost that two
months ago when he'd received a medical discharge
after the doctors determined that the knee injury he'd
sustained during a mission in the Middle East would

prevent him from performing his duties as a squad leader.

He drew in a deep steadying breath. How on earth could she even consider him as a likely candidate to father her child?

She didn't even know him. If she did, Katie would probably think twice about wanting his DNA to pass on to her offspring. His own father had never been in the picture and he doubted that his mother had even known which teenage boy had gotten her pregnant. For all Jeremiah knew about his own parents' backgrounds, he could carry a recessive gene for some kind of health or behavior problem, along with the ones for his physical characteristics.

He'd always thought little kids were great, but he'd never entertained the idea of fathering one. Far from it. He didn't have a clue about the role a dad was supposed to play in his child's life because the only dads he'd known were foster fathers. And they'd all viewed him as nothing more than a way to supplement their monthly income. They'd been compensated for providing a roof over his head, food in his mouth and to make sure he attended school regularly. They hadn't been paid to show him any kind of love and affection, nor had they cared to set an example of what a dad was supposed to be.

But then Katie wasn't asking him to remain in the picture past making a donation toward her cause. She wanted a baby without the encumbrances of a relationship, or the interference of the father trying to help her raise it.

He frowned. If he went along with her request, she would get the child she wanted, but what would he get out of the deal beyond the knowledge that he'd helped produce offspring?

He could insist that they make a baby the old-fashioned way and get the "no strings attached" fling that he wouldn't have considered possible with a woman like Katie. But as tempting as the thought was, he couldn't be that callous.

Rising to take their coffee mugs back into the kitchen, Jeremiah wondered how he could get her to reconsider visiting the sperm bank. It was a hell of a lot safer for her to become pregnant that way than it was for her to go around asking men she barely knew if they would father her child. Jeremiah shuddered to think what some jerk with less scruples would do if Katie asked him to help with her baby plan.

As he walked back into the great room to stretch out on the couch, he didn't want to think about why his gut burned from the very idea of her lying in the arms of another man, or carrying someone else's baby in her belly. He punched the couch cushion, muttered a curse that could have peeled chrome off a car bumper, then turned on his side to stare at the fire.

He had to find a way to convince her to visit that damn sperm bank and leave him the hell alone.

Four

A shaft of sunlight peeking through the curtains urged Katie to open her eyes. But looking around as she stretched, her heart stopped. Where was she? This wasn't her bedroom. This room was definitely a man's room with its heavy oak furniture, hunter-green bed linens and pictures of outdoor themes.

But as a woodsy, masculine scent teased her senses, the events of yesterday came rushing back. Asking Jeremiah to help her have a child. Taking him to the Dixie Ridge Clinic with a fishhook in his thumb. Having him strip her from the waist up after she'd fallen into the ice-cold creek. And making a fool of herself trying to explain why she couldn't wait any longer to have a baby.

''Oh, dear Lord, it wasn't a dream,'' she moaned, burrowing deeper under the thick comforter. The woodsy aroma surrounded her like a pair of strong arms and the memory of Jeremiah's kiss chased away all of her other thoughts.

Good heavens, the man had a lethal set of lips and he knew how to use them. Closing her eyes, Katie shivered as she remembered the feel of them settling over hers, the firmness of them as they moved over her mouth with practiced ease, and the taste of him as his tongue teased and explored. When she recalled how he'd pulled her to him, the memory of his hard arousal pressed to her lower stomach caused a lazy warmth to spread throughout her body and an aching heaviness to gather in her womb.

Her eyes flew open. Good grief, what was wrong with her? It wasn't like she'd never been kissed before. She touched her lips with her fingertips. But she could honestly say she'd never felt this kind of tension grip her from the mere memory of it.

Tossing back the covers, she started to get out of bed, but the sight of her laundered and neatly folded clothes, along with a Marine Corps T-shirt, lying at the foot of the bed stopped her cold. Jeremiah had washed her jeans and underthings.

Her cheeks heated and she had to take several deep breaths in order to stop the fluttering in her stomach. Last night he'd seen her breasts, and this morning he'd washed her panties. Would this nightmare ever end?

Wondering if there was a way to escape the cabin without having to face him again, Katie quickly changed out of his sweat suit and into her own clothes. As she slipped the T-shirt over her head, the woodsy scent of him surrounded her once again and caused her heart to skip several beats.

She prayed that she'd be able to get across the ford to her SUV, change the tire and make it back to Dixie Ridge without running into him. If she could do that, she promised the heavens above that she would never again be as impulsive as she'd been in the past twenty-four hours. What had she been thinking when she drove up Piney Knob to ask a man that she barely knew to be the sperm donor for her child?

When she opened the door and tentatively stepped out into the hall, she listened for any sound that indicated where Jeremiah might be. But the only thing she heard was the ticking of the antique clock on the mantel in the great room.

Maybe he'd gone fishing and facing him wouldn't be an issue. Feeling confident that she wouldn't have to suffer any further humiliation, Katie opened the front door and walked out onto the porch.

"I see you found your clothes."

Her heart skittered to a halt, then thumped in her chest like a bass drum in a marching band. "Y-yes. Thank you."

Jeremiah was sitting on a bench at one end of the porch, tying feathers to fishhooks. "You're going to have to get a new tire," he said, pointing toward her SUV parked close to his motorcycle. "When I changed it, I found a big gash in the sidewall. It's my guess, you scraped the sharp end of a submerged tree limb carried along by the rising water."

"You're probably right," she said, inching her way toward the steps. She needed to leave before she found some other bizarre way to embarrass herself in front of this man. "I appreciate everything you've done, but I'll be going now. I've bothered you enough."

"Don't you want to stick around and hear what I've decided?"

"About what?" she asked cautiously. His expression gave nothing away, but there was something in his tone that caused her senses to come to full alert.

"Your fertility problem," he said calmly.

Katie spun around so fast, she came close to falling off the edge of the porch. "But you said—"

He shrugged. "I gave it some thought and I've changed my mind." Setting the fly he'd been tying on the little wooden table in front of him, he moved it out of the way, then stood up. "Let's go inside. We can talk about it over coffee."

If she'd thought her heart was pounding before, it couldn't hold a candle to the hammering it was doing now. By the time they were seated at the trestle table in the kitchen, she wasn't altogether sure she hadn't misunderstood Jeremiah.

"You're going to help me have a child?" she asked cautiously.

He took a sip of his coffee, then setting the mug down, nodded. "I spent most of the night thinking about it, and if you're agreeable, then yes, I'll help you."

"Agreeable?" She didn't like the sound of that. "Just what would I be agreeing to?"

"I want joint custody," he said, smoothing the tape around the gauze Dr. Braden had wrapped around his left thumb. When he looked at her, he shrugged. "This will be the only child I ever have. I intend to be part of his life."

"Or her," Katie corrected him. "There's a fifty percent chance the baby will be a girl."

His smile sent goose bumps shimmering over her skin. "Point taken."

She nibbled on her lower lip as she considered what he said. It wasn't an unreasonable request. It just had never occurred to her that he might want to participate in raising her child.

"I suppose we could work out—"

He held up his hand. "Before you agree, you'd better hear me out."

"You have more stipulations?" she asked incredulously.

"Just one."

Something about his expression made her apprehensive. "Why do I get the idea I'm not going to like your next demand?"

He shrugged. "You never know. You might enjoy it."

A fresh wave of goose bumps slid along her arms and every instinct in her being told her to turn and run as far and fast as she possibly could in the opposite direction. Instead, she swallowed hard and asked, "What is it?"

"If I'm going to help you conceive this child, it will have to be the old-fashioned way," he said calmly.

Katie gulped. "You mean we'd—"

He nodded. "I'd make love to you until you became pregnant."

Feeling as if her world had just been turned upside down, Katie rose to her feet to pace the length of the kitchen. If she wanted a child, which she did, she'd have to sleep with Jeremiah Gunn?

The very thought of having him hold her in his arms while he buried his body deep inside of hers sent a shiver of longing up her spine and caused a heavy tightening in her lower belly. And that wasn't a good sign. Not at all.

If she felt this level of tension at the thought of making love with him, could she avoid becoming emotionally involved? Didn't two people coming together to create a new life develop a connection? Some kind of life-long bond?

Maybe if she reasoned with him, he'd see the wisdom in not taking that chance. "But it's not necessary. It's much more efficient and less complicated for you to visit the clinic and—"

"No, Katie." He stood up and walked over to stand in front of her. Placing his hands on her shoulders, his gaze held hers captive. "I'm a fully functioning male, and perfectly capable of taking care of the insemination myself. No offense to Dr. Braden, but his services will only be needed for the pregnancy and birth, not the conception."

Blushing all the way to the roots of her hair, she took a deep breath. "Are you sure you won't change your mind about this?"

"Positive."

She rubbed at her suddenly aching temples. "This isn't how I had everything planned. I'll need to think it over before I give you an answer."

He smiled as he cupped her cheek with his large palm. "You do that, honey." Leaning forward, he brushed her lips with his. "Take your time and weigh all of your options very carefully. I'm sure you'll come to the right decision."

At the same time Jeremiah slid his hands from her shoulders to her back, he covered her lips with his and coaxed her to open for him. Katie's eyes drifted shut as she parted for him, giving him access to the sensitive recesses within, allowing him to once again show her the mastery of his kiss.

As he explored her with a tenderness that brought tears to her eyes, he cupped her bottom with his hand and pulled her more fully against him. The feel of his strong arousal pressing into her soft, lower belly caused her knees to tremble and she had to wrap her arms around his waist to steady herself.

When she tentatively touched her tongue to his, a groan rumbled up from deep in his chest, sending tingles of excitement to every cell in her being. But when he lifted her to slide his leg between her thighs, the heated sensations it created in the most feminine part of her made Katie feel as if she'd go up in flames. Clinging to him to keep from going into total meltdown, her heart raced and she wasn't sure she'd ever breathe again when he moved his leg to create a delicious friction that was both thrilling and frightening in its intensity.

Panic quickly began to replace desire and she pushed against his chest. She needed to get away from him in order to think about what she might be getting herself into if she actually agreed to his terms.

When Jeremiah leisurely broke the kiss and released her, she quickly stepped back. "I…have to…get to work."

He brushed a strand of hair from her cheek. "Think about what you want and what I'm demanding, Katie." Leaning forward, he pressed a kiss to her forehead. "You can give me your answer whenever you're completely sure of what you want to do."

If she'd been able to find her voice, she'd have told him she wouldn't be able to think of anything else. Instead, she turned and left the house without a backward glance.

As she drove down Piney Knob, she did her best to keep her mind on steering her SUV around the hairpin turns and off of Jeremiah's offer. He was willing to make her dream of having a child come true, but at a price she wasn't sure she'd be able to pay. If her reaction to his kiss was anything to go by, she had a feeling that it would be downright impossible to keep her perspective and not become emotionally involved.

Sighing heavily, she parked the Explorer in her driveway, then reached in the glove box to remove the brochure Dr. Braden had given her yesterday. Maybe the Lancaster Sperm Bank wasn't as undesirable an option as she'd first thought.

When Jeremiah walked into the Blue Bird several days later, he had two things on his mind—seeing if Harv wanted to test out the new flies he had made while waiting for his thumb to heal, and watching Katie. For the past week, he'd found himself counting the hours until it was time to ride his motorcycle down the mountain to have lunch with Harv. And each day, Jeremiah spent less time listening to the older man lament his inability to find a suitable partner to help with his fishing and hunting business, and more time observing Katie.

After she walked out of his cabin the morning he'd outlined his requirements for helping her become pregnant, she'd studiously avoided any contact with him beyond taking his order and serving his food. That should have pleased him, considering he'd spent the entire night before their talk trying to figure a way to get her to take him out of the running for daddy candidates. So why did the fact that he'd obviously been successful irritate the hell out of him?

"How long are you gonna keep moon-eyein' that girl like you'd like to make her your next meal? Why don't you just ask her for a date and be done with it?"

When Jeremiah turned his full attention on Harv, the man was grinning like a damn fool. "What the hell's wrong with you, Harv? I'm not interested in Katie or any other woman."

"Sure." Harv laughed so hard Jeremiah expected him to fall off his chair. "Whatever you say, boy."

"She's not my type." Jeremiah barely resisted the urge to throttle the old goat when he noticed several of the Blue Bird's other patrons turning to stare at them.

"What's so funny, Harv?" Katie asked, smiling when she walked over to their table.

"It was just somethin' Jeremiah said," Harv answered, wiping his eyes. He looked like the cat that swallowed the canary when he slapped Jeremiah on the shoulder. "Sometimes this boy can be a real hoot."

Jeremiah was tempted more than ever to reach across the table and grab Harv by his scrawny throat. Instead he offered a bland smile. "Harv is the one cracking jokes today."

Nodding, her smile disappeared when she looked his way. "What can I get for you today, Jeremiah?"

Why did her sudden mood change bother him? Wasn't that what he wanted? Hadn't he made her that offer to scare her away?

"I'll take today's special and a glass of iced tea," he said automatically.

She jotted his order on the pad of paper she held, then turned to walk away. As if it were an afterthought, she called over her shoulder, "I'll bring it and your tea right out."

Once she was out of hearing range, Harv stared at him wide-eyed. "What in tarnation did you do to get Katie's bloomers in a bunch?"

"What makes you think she's upset with me?" Jeremiah asked cautiously.

Harv shook his head. "I've known Katie all her life and if she ain't bothered about somethin', I'll eat my hat and give you ten minutes to draw a crowd to watch it." He looked thoughtful for a moment before adding, "For the past week she's been givin' you the evil eye. Sorta like you've got somethin' that's catchin'."

Before Jeremiah could respond to Harv's observation, Katie walked back over to set a plate piled high with fried chicken, mashed potatoes and black-eyed peas in front of him, then walked away without a word.

"See what I mean?" Harv asked. "Katie never fails to tell her customers to enjoy their meal. But she didn't say diddly squat to you just now."

"She's probably got her mind on something else," Jeremiah said evasively. He had a good idea what that "something" was, but he wasn't about to enlighten Harv.

Giving Jeremiah a skeptical look, Harv refrained from commenting further and picked up his fork to start shoveling food into his mouth.

Relieved to be left to his own thoughts, Jeremiah watched Katie move around behind the lunch counter as he took a bite of mashed potatoes and gravy. For all he tasted of the normally mouthwatering food, it might as well have been a pile of sawdust.

Why was he irritated by the fact that she was so obviously ignoring him? Hadn't that been the purpose behind his setting conditions when he'd agreed to help her have a baby?

After he'd devised his plan, he'd been sure Katie would find it so completely unacceptable that she'd abandon the idea of knowing the father of her baby and resort to the sperm bank to solve her problem. And the way she'd fled his cabin that morning a week ago, he had been certain he'd accomplished his goal. But he hadn't expected her to carry a grudge.

"You haven't heard a word I just said, have you?" Harv asked, interrupting Jeremiah's disturbing thoughts.

"Sorry, Harv." He turned his full attention on the older man. "What was that you were saying?"

"I asked if you've been thinkin' any more about puttin' down roots," Harv said, pushing his empty plate to the side and reaching for a bowl of blackberry cobbler. "You know, Ray Applegate's still lookin' to sell that cabin you're stayin' in."

"That's what you keep telling me." Jeremiah was much more comfortable with old Harv trying to talk him into staying around Dixie Ridge than he was discussing Katie's attitude toward him.

"Have you talked to Ray about what kind of price he's askin' for the place?" Harv asked around a mouthful of cobbler.

Jeremiah shook his head. "If I decide that I'm interested in sticking around for a while, I will. But not until then."

Conscious of every move Katie made, he knew immediately that she'd turned her attention in his direction. When their gazes met, he watched her say something to the cook through the window behind the counter, then start walking toward him.

"Here are your checks," she said, placing the two tickets on the table. "I hope you both enjoyed your meal." Looking nervous, she paused for a moment as if she had something more she'd like to say, then shaking her head, moved on to the next table.

"Well, I guess I'd better be gettin' back to work," Harv said, shoving his chair back. "I've got a beginner castin' class that starts up first thing in the mornin' and I need to get everything ready." Rising to his feet, he asked, "You wouldn't happen to know of anybody wantin' a job teachin' people to tie their own flies, would you?"

Harv was about as transparent as a window pane. The old guy had all but come out and asked if Jeremiah would become his partner in Piney Knob Outfitters.

"No, but if I run into anyone, I'll let you know," Jeremiah said, chuckling. He started to get up to follow Harv, but a hand resting lightly on his shoulder stopped him cold.

"Could you stay until the crowd thins out a bit more?" Katie asked, her tone barely above a whisper. "I need to talk to you."

Jeremiah froze, but he wasn't sure whether his reaction was from her quiet request, or the warmth of her soft hand through the fabric of his T-shirt. Looking over his shoulder, he almost groaned. Her head was so close that if he turned a little more and leaned forward, their lips would touch.

"It will only take a moment or two," she said, glancing toward Harv. Considering the older man's inclination for gossiping, Jeremiah could understand her reluctance to draw Harv's attention.

Unsure whether he should be glad she was no

longer ignoring him or run like hell, he ended up nodding. "Sure. I'll stick around."

She moved away a moment before Harv turned to
ask, "Ain't you leavin', too, Jeremiah?"

Thinking fast, Jeremiah shook his head. "That cobbler you had after your meal looked so good, I decided to try a bowl myself."

"You won't regret it," Harv said, grinning. "No-
body makes blackberry cobbler like Helen." Moving
on toward the cash register, he threw up his hand to
several of the other regulars. "See y'all later."

After Harv left it didn't take long for the lunch
crowd to thin out, leaving only Jeremiah and a couple
of other patrons. He watched Katie glance his way
several times, then square her shoulders and walk
around the counter toward his table.

"Thank you for waiting," she said, seating herself
in the chair across from him.

He shrugged. "Not a problem. What did you want
to talk about?"

"I've…reached a decision about your offer," she
said, clasping her hands into a knot on top of the table
in front of her. He watched her take a deep breath
before raising her gaze to meet his. "I think you know
that I want a baby more than anything. But—"

When she stopped to take a deep breath, Jeremiah
reached out to cover her hands with one of his. The
feel of her soft skin beneath his rough palm did
strange things to his insides and almost had him re-
gretting that they wouldn't be making love.

"It's all right, honey," he said, careful to keep his voice low. "Your decision to refuse my offer is understandable."

She gave him a look that made the hair on the back of his neck stand straight up. "That's not what I was trying to tell you."

His throat suddenly felt as if it had been filled with sand and he had to swallow several times to get words past his uncooperative vocal cords. "What are you trying to say, Katie?"

"I was going to tell you that although I want a child more than anything else in the world, I just can't bring myself to go to the sperm bank." The shy, blushing smile she sent his way caused his heart to hammer so hard against his ribs that he was sure it would break right through at any second. "Since you're my only other option, I've decided to accept your offer."

"Y-you're agreeing to my terms?" he croaked out, surprised that his voice worked at all.

She nodded. "Yes. I'm agreeing to share custody of our child and..." She blushed, fascinating him. "I'll make love to you until I become pregnant." Her cheeks turned a deeper shade of rose as she asked, "When would you like to start?"

Five

Jeremiah wasn't sure whether to get down on his hands and knees and thank the good Lord above that he'd get to make love to Katie, or cuss a blue streak over being caught in his own trap. Either way, he'd never dreamed that she would agree to his conditions.

"Katie, could you ring up Miss Millie and Homer's lunch ticket, while I start cleaning up back here?" the cook called from somewhere in the kitchen.

"I need to help Helen get ready to close for the day," she said, rising from the chair. "Could we meet late this afternoon to discuss this further?"

Jeremiah nodded as he got to his feet and followed her to the cash register. He needed to be by himself for a while anyway. It was going to take a little time to come to grips with what had taken place in the past few minutes. He also needed to think of a way to get out of the corner he'd boxed himself into.

"What time will you be ready to leave?" he asked, once she'd sent the old couple on their way. Digging into his pocket for money to pay his bill, he handed it to her, then shook his head when she started to hand him back his change. "Keep it."

"Since we're only open for breakfast and lunch, I'm usually out of here by three," she said, putting his tip into a jar on the counter. She gave him a smile that damn near knocked him to his knees, adding, "Anytime after that will be fine."

Nodding, Jeremiah started toward the door. "I'll be back then."

When he walked out of the Blue Bird and climbed onto his Harley, he checked his watch. He had a lot of thinking to do and only a couple of hours in which to do it.

As he rode his motorcycle out onto the road and across the bridge over Piney River, he tried to figure out just what had gone wrong with his plan, and how he'd gotten in over his head so damn fast. He'd been sure Katie would turn him down flat once she heard his conditions. But she hadn't.

Sweat popped out on his forehead. He'd always made it a point to take the proper precautions against making a woman pregnant. Was he really ready to make love to Katie with that purpose in mind?

The thought of holding her, loving her until she called his name as she found her release, caused his groin to tighten and had him steering the Harley to the side of the road. Killing the engine, he looked out over the scenic mountains surrounding Dixie Ridge as he mulled over everything.

Could he make love to Katie without becoming emotionally involved? Would he be able to keep things in perspective, knowing that his baby was growing inside her belly?

And what about the child? Raising a kid was a huge responsibility and one that he'd never intended to undertake. Was he ready to make that kind of commitment?

He knew Katie would be a wonderful mother, and there wasn't a doubt in his mind that she'd ever do to their child what his own mother had done to him. But could he be a good father, considering that he'd never really had a role model?

Jeremiah took a deep breath and started the motorcycle's powerful engine. He didn't have any more answers now than he had an hour ago.

But if he was nothing else, he *was* a man of his word. He'd told Katie that if she agreed to his conditions, he would help her have a baby. And although it scared the living hell out of him to think of what he might be getting himself into, he'd given her his word and that's exactly what he intended to do.

Now all they had left to decide was when and where to get started.

Katie's heart sped up when she heard Jeremiah's motorcycle coming down the road as she closed and locked the Blue Bird's door. There was no doubt in her mind it was him. Aside from the fact that there were only a couple of other men in Dixie Ridge who owned motorcycles, Jeremiah's had a distinct rumble the others didn't and the sound seemed to carry for miles.

When he pulled into the parking space in front of her, he turned off the engine, but didn't bother removing his mirrored sunglasses. "Are you ready?"

Her heart skipped several beats. "Ready for what?" Surely he didn't mean...

"I thought it might be best if we go up to my place so that we can talk in private." He nodded toward a couple of people waving to her as they entered the clinic across the road. "I doubt that you want anyone listening when we discuss our arrangement."

"Oh, of course not," she said shaking her head. "I'd rather keep it quiet for now." Why hadn't she thought of that?

He pointed to her head. "Do you have something to tie your hair back?"

Taking the scrunchy she used when she worked

from her pocket, Katie pulled the long strands back into a ponytail. "I'm glad I wear blue jeans and a T-shirt when I work instead of a uniform or a dress. Otherwise, it would make riding your motorcycle rather difficult."

She was babbling, but she couldn't seem to stop herself. She'd never been more excited, or nervous, in all of her thirty-four years than she was at that moment.

Once she had her hair secured, he motioned for her to put on the helmet strapped to the narrow leather seat. "Hop on and put your feet on these," he said, pointing to the shiny chrome pegs on either side of the motorcycle. "Then hold on to my waist."

Katie placed her hands loosely at his waist when Jeremiah took hold of the handle grips and the Harley rumbled to life. But when the motorcycle started to move, she wrapped her arms around him, plastered herself to his back and hung on for dear life.

The engine was so loud she couldn't hear herself think, but as they rode out of town and turned onto the road leading up the side of Piney Knob, she found that the experience wasn't nearly as frightening as she'd thought it would be. Holding on to Jeremiah's solid strength, while she observed the easy way he controlled the big machine, soon had her relaxing and enjoying the ride. The wind in her face and the warmth of his big body against hers felt wonderful, and by the time he parked the motorcycle next to his

porch some twenty minutes later, she was almost disappointed that the ride hadn't been longer.

Switching off the engine, he waited for her to take
off the helmet and get off the back of the Harley, then
using the toe of his boot, lowered the chrome stand.
"You've never ridden before, have you?"

She shook her head. "How could you tell?"

Laughing, he rubbed his side. "I think I have a
couple of cracked ribs."

"Please tell me you're joking." She thought he
was, but now that they were truly alone, she was
fighting a major case of nerves and her sense of humor wasn't quite up to par.

He stopped laughing, got off the motorcycle and
reaching out, cupped her cheek in his large palm.
"Lighten up, honey. We're just here to talk. Nothing
is going to happen until we've discussed our agreement and made a few decisions."

"Decisions?" she asked, confused. "You were
quite clear with your stipulations and I agreed to
them. Didn't that cover everything?"

"Not by a long shot." He placed his hand to her
back to guide her toward the porch. "We have to
decide when, where and how often we're going to try
to make you pregnant."

Katie felt herself blushing from the top of her head
to the soles of her feet. She'd only made the decision
this morning to go along with his terms, and Jeremiah's frank assessment of what they needed to talk

over hadn't even occurred to her. But he was right. They did need to discuss the details, no matter how embarrassing it became talking about the number of times they would be making love.

"And before we go any further with this, I want you to know that other than some cartilage missing out of my left knee, I'm healthy," he said as they climbed the steps. "I haven't been with a woman in over a year and I've always been conscientious about protection. But if you'd like me to go for an examination, I will."

"N-no, that won't be necessary." Good heavens, he was thinking of all kinds of things that hadn't occurred to her. Before he had a chance to ask, she added, "In case you're wondering, I'm healthy, too."

Once they were seated side by side on the porch swing, he rested his arm along the back. "It's entirely up to you, but I think when we make love it should be here at the cabin. It's more private and your neighbors are less likely to wonder what's going on. That might keep the gossip down in the beginning, but I'm not sure how we'll head that off once you start showing."

"That won't be a problem." She watched a hummingbird buzz around the bright red feeder at the far end of the porch. Jeremiah had given the logistics more thought than she had, but she'd already come up with what she intended to tell everyone when she became pregnant. "I'm just going to tell the truth—that I decided to have a baby before it was too late."

He reached over to thread his long, masculine fingers with hers, then gave her hand a gentle squeeze. "We'll tell them that *we* made that decision, Katie. I'm not letting you take all the heat. This may have been your idea, but he'll be my kid, too. From now on, we're in this together. Okay?"

Turning her head to stare at him, she saw the determination in his chocolate-brown eyes. "Thank you."

"See? That wasn't so difficult." His smile made her feel warm all over. "Next question. When do you want to start trying to get pregnant?"

She took a deep breath and fought the urge to blush yet again. "I think…the sooner the better. I bought a book explaining the signs of fertility. It said that I might not become pregnant right away, but that certain times are better than others. I've already started recording my temperature each morning and keeping a chart to help me determine when—"

"Forget the record keeping, Katie." He turned loose of her hand as he shook his head, then turning her to face him, wrapped his arms around her and pulled her to him. "If you're going to keep charts and make graphs you might as well go to the sperm bank."

"But the book says—"

"To hell with the book." His lips brushed hers. "It

makes getting you pregnant too clinical and takes all the fun out of making love.''

A shiver skipped up her spine. ''F-fun?''

He nodded. ''Just because we'll be making love in order for you to become pregnant doesn't mean we can't enjoy ourselves.''

Before she could find her voice, Jeremiah's mouth settled over hers and she forgot all about fertility books, or taking her temperature and charting the results. His firm lips were moving over hers with such care that it stole her breath and robbed her of all rational thought.

When he coaxed her to open for him, the feel of his tongue slipping inside, the way he explored and teased, sent heat shimmering through every part of her. Bringing her arms up to encircle his shoulders, she clung to his solid strength as Jeremiah took his time showing her that he meant every word he'd said.

Katie threaded her fingers in the thick, raven-black hair at the nape of his neck and completely surrendered herself to his slow, sensual assault. Heat flowed through her veins to gather at the most feminine part of her when his hand slid from her back, then up her side to cover her breast.

Her quiet moan of pleasure seemed to encourage him, and he moved his thumb to chafe the hardened nipple through the layers of her clothing. Swirling ribbons of intense sensation threaded their way throughout her being and an empty ache began to form deep within her lower belly.

"See what I mean, honey?" He kissed his way to the pulse hammering at the base of her throat. "Making a baby is going to be pure pleasure for both of us."

"I…hope…you're right." Her heart stopped, then took off at a gallop. Had she really said that?

His deep chuckle sent a shaft of longing straight to her core. "Leave it to me, honey. I'll make sure it is." She felt his chest expand as he took a deep breath, then set her away from him. "The Blue Bird is closed on the weekends, isn't it?"

"Yes. We're just a five-day-a-week, breakfast and lunch operation," she said, straightening her T-shirt.

"Did you have anything planned from tomorrow after you get off work until Monday morning?"

She shook her head. "Not really. I was going to work on a quilt I'm making to sell in one of the gift shops in Gatlinburg. But that was all."

"Good." He stood up and held out his hand to help her to her feet. "Do you have a backpack or a gym bag that I could tie on the back of my Harley?" When she nodded, he smiled. "Pack some clothes and take them to work with you tomorrow morning. I'll pick up the bag when I come down for lunch, then come back for you after you get off work tomorrow afternoon."

"You want me to spend the weekend?" Katie gulped. "Here? With you?"

"If we're going to be successful at this, it might be a good idea if we spent a little time together," he said, dryly.

She had to force herself to breathe. "But it seems so…soon."

He shrugged as he linked their fingers and started down the porch steps toward his motorcycle. "You were the one who said the sooner we got started, the better."

Katie's heart thumped so hard she was surprised it didn't jump right out of her chest. "But I'd planned on charting my temperature for a month in order to find the best time to try."

Smiling, he shook his head as he put his leg over the motorcycle, then used the heel of his boot to flip the stand up. "That's way too clinical. Remember?" He waited for her to climb onto the seat behind him. "We can chart your temperature if you don't get pregnant right away. Until then, we'll just relax, have fun and let nature take its course."

He started the motorcycle, ending any further conversation, and as they rode back down Piney Knob, Katie suddenly found herself second-guessing her decision. She wanted a baby more than anything else and she'd based her agreement with Jeremiah on the old adage that the end would justify the means. But she'd thought the "means" would be nothing more than a quick coupling in order to fertilize one of her aging eggs. She hadn't counted on him insisting that they enjoy the experience.

Holding on to him as he guided the Harley around a hairpin turn, she shivered when she felt his back and shoulder muscles flex beneath the stretched fabric of his black T-shirt. Until now, she'd studiously avoided thinking about Jeremiah holding her to his nude body, or feeling him fill her with his strength. She hadn't even allowed herself to think of their encounters as lovemaking.

But if his kisses and her reaction to them were any indication, their coming together was going to be a whole lot more than quick and efficient. The words exciting, erotic and explosive came to mind, and those were just off the top of her head. If she let herself, she was sure she'd think of more.

Katie gave herself a mental shake. She wasn't going to pursue that train of thought. She needed to focus on the future and being able to hold her own precious baby in her arms, not dwell on how pleasurable being held in Jeremiah's arms for the conception might be.

The next day, Jeremiah sat on his Harley in front of the Blue Bird waiting for Katie to get off work. When he'd picked her up yesterday to take her to his cabin so they could discuss the details of their agreement, he'd had every intention of being so candid about their lovemaking that she'd think twice about going through with her baby-making scheme. But the minute he'd seen her standing there waiting on him, he'd forgotten all about that, and thought of nothing but how good it would feel making slow, passionate love to her.

Wondering if he'd lost his mind, he shook his head. She wasn't even the type of woman he normally preferred. He liked his women shamelessly sexy and as uninhibited and willing as he was. But Katie wasn't any of those things. She was sweet, shy about her body and blushed at the mere mention of anything intimate.

Yet, all he could think about was holding her to him, sinking himself deep inside of her and watching as she came apart when she found her pleasure. And that was what amazed him.

Unless he missed his guess, Katie wasn't all that experienced in the ways of bedroom bliss. So why, for the first time in his life, was he looking forward to teaching a woman how to make love?

And that was just the tip of the iceberg. He'd lain awake most of last night thinking about the baby they were going to create. What would it be like watching Katie's belly grow round with his child? Would their lovemaking produce a boy or a girl? Would the baby look like Katie or be a carbon copy of him?

Hell, he'd even gone so far as to start thinking about what it would be like to be a dad. Was he capable of making the right decisions? Could he guide a child along the right path? Would he be able to let down his guard, love the little guy like he deserved to be loved, and risk not being loved in return?

Jeremiah had spent his entire life avoiding rejection whenever possible. And the best way he'd found to do that was not to set himself up for it to begin with. If he didn't get too close to anyone, he couldn't be hurt. But the baby he and Katie intended to make would be his own flesh and blood. Wouldn't that be different?

It hadn't been for his mother. But then, Anita Gunn had only been half Katie's age when she'd given birth to him. And she'd only been a few years older than that when she'd abandoned him in a busy discount store, never to be seen or heard from again.

Jeremiah released a frustrated breath as he watched Katie close and lock the front door of the Blue Bird. He had a hell of a lot more questions than he had answers. But he'd given his word, and as far as he was concerned that was as good as any iron-clad contract a high-priced attorney could draw up.

"Are you ready to go?" he asked when she slowly walked toward him.

"I guess so," she said, reaching up to tighten the puffy red tieback holding her long, dark hair in a ponytail.

The hesitancy he detected in her soft voice and the apprehensive look in her blue-green eyes caused his gut to twist. Reaching out, he put his arm around her waist to draw her to his side. "We don't have to do this, honey. If you've changed your mind, and would rather make a visit to the sperm bank, I'll understand."

She took a deep breath, then smiling, shook her head. "I haven't changed my mind. I still want you to be my baby's daddy."

He stared at her for several long seconds. Every time she mentioned wanting him to father her child, a feeling he couldn't explain filled his chest.

"Are you sure?" He had to know that this was what she really wanted.

"Yes." There was no hesitation this time, and the determination in her eyes told him that she meant what she said.

Releasing her, he started to tell her to climb on the motorcycle behind him when an older woman waved as she got out of her car at the clinic across the street. "Hi, Katie. How have you been?"

"Oh, great," Katie muttered as she lifted her hand to return the woman's greeting.

"Who's that?" Jeremiah asked, watching the woman hurry toward them.

"Sadie Jenkins, the biggest gossip in Dixie Ridge."

Jeremiah chuckled. "I thought Harv had the corner on that market."

"Who do you think gave Harv lessons? He's a rank

amateur compared to his wife," she whispered, shaking her head.

"Have you heard from your mother lately?" Sadie asked as she approached.

Jeremiah noticed the knuckles on Katie's hand turned white where she gripped the strap on her shoulder bag. "I talked to her last week," Katie answered the woman with a smile. "Mom said that she and dad were having the time of their lives helping Carol Ann with the quads."

Sadie nodded, but she clearly wasn't listening to a word Katie said. The woman was too busy staring Jeremiah up and down. "You must be the young man Harv keeps telling me about."

"The name's Jeremiah Gunn," he said as he held out his hand. "Harv and I have lunch together almost every day." Jeremiah didn't bother rising from the motorcycle. He didn't plan on talking to the woman that long.

Grinning, Sadie shook his hand. "Harv said you were a strappin' young buck, but he didn't tell me how handsome you are. No wonder Katie's standin' here talkin' to you instead of goin' home to work on one of her quilts."

Jeremiah watched Katie roll her eyes and from the expression on her face he'd bet good money she was only a second or two away from telling the woman to mind her own business. "Katie and I were just about to take a ride up Piney Knob to do a little trout fishing," he lied, hoping to head off a confrontation. "Harv's been telling me that I could learn a thing or two from Katie about casting accuracy."

"I would think so," Sadie said, nodding so vigorously her salt-and-pepper curls bounced. "Katie's the Powder-Puff champion and has been for years."

"That's what I've heard." He made a show of checking his watch. "I really hate to cut this short, Mrs. Jenkins. But I'd like to get in as much fishing as I can before it gets too late."

Sadie laughed. "You anglers are all alike. Harv would stand out in the middle of a stream from sunup to sundown if he could." She looked thoughtful for a moment, then her face lit up like a kid's at Christmas. "Why don't the two of you come over to our place for supper tonight?"

"Thanks, Sadie, but I don't really think we'll have time," Katie said, looking more than a little frustrated.

"Pish posh!" Sadie shook her head. "I won't take 'no' for an answer." She gave Katie a hug, then smiled at Jeremiah. "I'll expect you two at our house about five-thirty."

They watched the woman walk back across the street to enter the clinic. "Looks like we're stuck having to eat with the Jenkinses this evening," Jeremiah finally said.

"It's going to be a *very* short evening," Katie

stated flatly. She didn't look or sound in the least bit pleased.

Figuring they only had a couple of hours before going over to the Jenkins' place, Jeremiah shrugged. "We might as well hang around town if we're going to be dining with Harv and Sadie tonight, then head up to the cabin after supper. What do you say we take a ride over to Piney Falls and back?"

"Fine with me."

As soon as Katie climbed onto the seat behind him, Jeremiah started the Harley and steered it out of the parking space. He smiled when she plastered herself to his back and wrapped her arms around his waist in a bear hug. Riding with him might be frightening to her, but he was beginning to enjoy having her on the back of his motorcycle.

"Thanks for having us over for dinner," Jeremiah said, shaking hands with Harv, while Katie suffered another hug from Sadie. "I'll see you at the Blue Bird for lunch on Monday."

Harv pumped his hand so hard, Jeremiah wouldn't have been surprised if he ended up with a sprained wrist. "You want to cast a line or two tomorrow morning?"

"I can't go fishing tomorrow, Harv," Jeremiah said, thinking fast. "I have some things I need to get done around the cabin."

He watched Harv wink at his wife. "All righty. Let's make it Sunday after church service."

"Sorry," Jeremiah said, shaking his head. "I have plans then, too." As a way to appease the old guy, he added, "Why don't we plan a trip for Monday afternoon. I've been wanting to try my luck on the Little River."

"Sounds good to me," Harv said happily.

"Well, I need to get Katie home before it gets dark," Jeremiah said, carefully omitting who's place he was referring to—his or hers.

"Tell your mother I said hello the next time you talk to her," Sadie said, grinning.

Katie nodded. "I will."

As they walked down the steps and over to his motorcycle parked in the driveway, Jeremiah noticed that Katie looked as if she was going to explode. "So what do you think she'll be telling everyone about us?" he asked, careful to keep his voice low as he lifted his leg over the back of the Harley and sat down.

"That you and I are either having a torrid affair, or getting ready to take a trip down the aisle." Katie straddled the seat behind him. "And the first person she's going to tell will be my mother."

"But I thought she said for you to tell your mom hello the next time the two of you talked."

Chuckling, he raised an eyebrow at the unladylike word Katie muttered as she rested her hands at his waist. "Sadie won't let her shirttail hit her backside before she's on the phone with my mother in California. By the time we get to the edge of town, she'll be telling Mom all about me riding around town on your motorcycle with you, and that we're probably going up Piney Knob to your cabin to do no telling what."

"But I told her I was taking you home."

"Yes, but by the time Sadie puts her spin on it—"

"I'll be whisking you up the mountain where we'll run naked through the woods and make mad passionate love on the banks of the stream behind the cabin," he guessed.

"Something like that." She rested her head against the back of his shoulder. "I can't wait to hear what she has to say when I become pregnant."

Jeremiah didn't say anything as he started the Harley and steered it out onto the road leading up to the cabin. He couldn't. He was suddenly too angry to speak without using words that weren't fit for a lady's ears.

What Katie had just told him didn't set well at all. Sadie Jenkins could say what the hell she wanted about him, but the woman had better not start spreading rumors about Katie.

If she did, Sadie would have him to deal with. And he didn't think the old bat wanted to go there. Just ask any of the men serving under him who'd been stupid enough to question his orders—Jeremiah Gunn could be one mean son of a gun when the occasion called for it.

And as far as he was concerned, gossiping about a decent woman like Katie was more than enough provocation.

Six

Katie's heart skipped several beats when Jeremiah closed the door and locked it behind them. She'd been alone in the cabin with him before, but that had been different. That night she'd almost drowned, had been in danger of suffering hypothermia, and he hadn't yet agreed to help her get pregnant. But knowing that was the very reason for her being here now made her a little anxious.

"What do we do first?" she asked. Not having any experience at this sort of thing, she had no idea how to proceed.

"Nothing." He tossed his keys on the end table beside the burgundy leather couch. "We need to talk about this a little more."

"But I thought we settled everything yesterday." Her heart felt as if it had come up in her throat. Was he going to renege on their arrangement, or add more stipulations that she'd have to agree to?

He shook his head. "I've been in the military for almost twenty years and I'd forgotten how destructive small-town gossip can be. I don't like the idea of you being the subject of the Dixie Ridge gossip mill."

Katie sat on one end of the couch. "You mean Sadie?"

"And others," he added, nodding. "You know when you become pregnant and the word spreads, the old biddies are going to keep the phone lines hot, speculating about why we aren't married."

She shrugged. "I decided on the ride up here that, although I don't like being the center of attention, I don't care what anyone says. I made the choice to have a baby and that's what I'm going to do. It's none of their business. Besides, Sadie doesn't have any room to gossip or spread rumors about anyone else."

"What do you mean?"

Katie grinned. "I have it on good authority that she and Harv were the talk of Dixie Ridge before they got married. And forty years ago, society wasn't nearly as forgiving about these things as they are now. It took several years for people around here to forget that she and Harv's oldest son was almost three when they finally married."

Jeremiah frowned. "But I thought you were concerned about her calling your mother."

"I was at first. But not anymore." She took the scrunchy from her hair and ran her fingers through it to loosen some of the tangles. "I would rather have the opportunity to tell my mom and dad about my decision before Sadie does, but I know that's not going to happen. So I don't intend to worry about it."

He looked incredulous. "You really want a baby that much, don't you?"

"Yes, I do." Standing up, she walked over to look out the picture window at the mountains beyond. She needed to make him understand just how important it was for her to have her own child before it was too late. "I know it's probably going to sound like I lack ambition by today's standards because I don't want to move away from Dixie Ridge and have a career. But I've never wanted that. For as far back as I can remember my dream in life has always been to be a wife and mother."

"There isn't a damn thing wrong with that, honey." He came over to stand behind her. "And I don't think it shows a lack of ambition." Placing his hands on her shoulders, he began to massage the tension gripping her. "If anything, it's a good indication of your courage and dedication to realizing your dream." His warm breath feathered over her ear as he leaned close. "Although I don't have anything to compare it to, from what I've heard, being a mother is a lot more than a nine-to-five job. It's twenty-four hours a day, seven days a week for a good eighteen to twenty years. If you ask me, that's a hell of a lot more ambitious than most careers.''

His understanding words and warm palms were comforting and she felt her tension begin to drain away. ''When I was in my late teens and early twenties, I used to think that I'd meet someone, get married and have a houseful of babies to love and care for. But when I reached my thirtieth birthday, I finally had to face the fact that wasn't going to happen. That's when I gave up on having a husband and settled on having a family instead.''

''What makes you think that's no longer a possibility?''

She laughed. ''Men aren't attracted to a woman as tall, or even taller than they are. Nor do they want one who outweighs them by fifty pounds.''

His hands stilled. ''Who told you a stupid thing like that?''

''I didn't have to be told.'' She shrugged one shoulder. ''Even if my height wasn't an issue, I know that men aren't attracted to a woman who resembles the Michelin Man or the Pillsbury Doughboy.''

He turned her to face him, and the scowl on his face caused her to take a step back. His arms closed around her waist to impede her retreat.

''Where did you come up with the harebrained idea that you aren't attractive?'' Pulling her forward, he rested his forehead against hers. "Some of us like our women tall and well-rounded."

She couldn't believe the direction their conversation had taken. She'd come to terms with her body type, accepted that she would always be full-figured, and at times even found it to her advantage, like the night she'd fallen into the flooded creek. If she'd been of a smaller stature, she'd have most likely been swept downstream and over Piney Falls. But she never dreamed she'd be discussing it with a man, the way she was with Jeremiah.

"There's a difference between being well-rounded and looking like a defensive tackle for the Tennessee Titans football team," she said breathlessly.

"Honey, if you'll remember, I've seen you without your clothes," he said, grinning. "And there's no way in hell anyone could mistake you for a football player."

Her cheeks grew warm. "You were supposed to forget about that."

"I can't," he said, sliding his hands down to her hips. He pulled her forward and the hard ridge of his arousal pressed to her lower belly caused her pulse to beat double-time. "Do you feel that? Just thinking about the night I had to take off your clothes makes me hard."

"I didn't think you…were the least bit…affected," she said, finding it hard to breathe.

"Oh, I was affected all right. I didn't get any sleep

at all that night. Do you know why?'' When she
shook her head, he lifted her chin with his index finger until their gazes met. ''I couldn't stop thinking
about how beautiful you are, and how much I wanted
to hold your soft curves to me as I buried myself deep
inside of you.''

Katie couldn't have forced her vocal cords to work
if her life depended on it.

Smiling, he lowered his head. ''Never doubt that
you're desirable, honey.'' His mouth covered hers for
a brief kiss. ''But in case you still have any doubts,
I intend to spend the entire weekend showing you just
how much.''

When he traced her lips with his tongue, then deepened the kiss, tingles of excitement skipped over
every nerve in her body and Katie thought she just
might go into total meltdown. Her knees felt as if
they'd turned to rubber and the blood in her veins to
warm honey.

He threaded his fingers in her hair to hold her captive as he tenderly stroked her inner recesses. Tasting
his passion sent her pulse racing and caused her temperature to soar. He was showing her that he meant
what he said, and she was left with no doubt that he
did find her very attractive.

Slowly easing the pressure of his mouth on hers,
he broke the kiss. ''I want you so much I can't think
straight.'' His lips brushed over her cheek and closed

eyelids. "Let's go into the bedroom and I'll show you how much."

"Should I change into my nightshirt?" she asked, suddenly feeling extremely inadequate.

His deep chuckle close to her ear sent a shiver of anticipation racing up her spine. "What for? I'll just end up taking it off of you." Releasing her, he took her hand in his. "When I make love to you, I don't want anything between us. I want to feel every inch of your beautiful body against mine."

Katie couldn't think of a thing to say as he led her across the great room and down the hall. His provocative words, the promising smile on his firm male lips and the heat in his dark brown eyes made words unnecessary.

When he opened the bedroom door, then stood back for her to enter, her heart thumped against her ribs erratically and she wasn't sure that her legs would support her as she walked into the room. She briefly noticed the small gym bag that she'd given Jeremiah at lunchtime sitting on the dresser. Goose bumps shimmered over her skin when she thought about the nightshirt she'd packed and the statement he'd made about there being no need for her to put it on.

Turning to face him, her breath caught. He was already tugging his navy T-shirt from the waistband of his well-worn jeans.

Suddenly more nervous than she could ever remember, she tried to decide if she should follow suit.

Before she had the chance to recall what she'd seen in movies and read in books, he pulled his shirt over his head and tossed it onto a chair by the dresser.

He walked over to the bedside table, switched on the lamp, then turned to face her. "Let me," he said, moving her hands away from the hem of her pink knit shirt. "I'm going to enjoy taking your clothes off and kissing every inch of you."

"You don't have to seduce me," she said, desperately trying to keep sight of their purpose. She needed to remember she was going to make love to him to conceive a child, not complicate matters with an emotional connection neither of them wanted.

He shook his head. "Honey, this isn't a seduction." He slid his hands under the tail of her shirt and up along her ribs, taking the garment with him. When he slipped it off and tossed it on the chair with his, he smiled. "This is foreplay."

She caught her breath. "But it's not necessary—"

"Yes, it is." He put his index finger to her lips to silence the rest of her protest. "I want you to forget that we're trying to make you pregnant and enjoy what we're doing."

"I don't think…I'll be able to do that," she said, feeling more breathless by the second.

"Sure you can," he said, wrapping his arms around her. He splayed his hands on her bare back as he kissed his way from her shoulder to her ear. "Just close your eyes and let me make you feel good, Katie.''

With his smooth baritone lulling her, his hands caressing her body, and his lips kissing her sensitized skin, the tension inside her seemed to transform into something entirely different. She suddenly felt warm all over and she forgot all the reasons she shouldn't fall under his sensual spell.

"That's it, honey," he said apparently sensing the change within her. "Concentrate on how I'm making you feel."

Closing her eyes, she did as he instructed and it came as no small surprise when he pulled her forward that he'd removed her bra. The feel of her breasts pressed to his hard chest sent tiny electric charges throughout her body and had her forgetting anything but the man holding her within the circle of his arms.

"You feel so damn good," he said, his tone lower and more husky than normal.

"So...do you." Drawing her next breath was becoming increasingly more difficult with each passing second.

He kissed her temple, her cheek, then fused their lips in a kiss that caused stars to flash behind her eyelids and liquid fire to flow through her veins. Wave after wave of heat spread to every cell of her being and Katie found herself having to cling to his hard biceps to keep from falling at his feet.

Her mind seemed to shut down to any and all

thought as her senses were filled with Jeremiah. His woodsy masculine scent, the taste of his passion, and the contrast of his hard maleness to her much softer, feminine form enticed her to get closer. When she put her arms around his waist to explore the well-developed muscles of his broad back with her fingertips, a groan rumbled up from deep in his chest. The sound vibrated against her lips and seemed to create an answering quiver deep inside of her.

"Let's get the rest of these clothes off while we're still capable of standing," he said, raining tiny kisses from her cheek to her ear.

Opening her eyes, Katie's hands trembled as she started to do as he suggested, but he shook his head. "I'll take care of it, honey."

He bent down to remove her sandals, then his boots and socks. Straightening, he gave her a smile that curled her toes as he reached for the button at the top of her jeans. Once he worked it free, he quickly lowered the zipper and pushed her jeans and panties down her thighs to her ankles. At his encouragement, she stepped out of her clothes and used her foot to nudge them aside.

She had to fight the urge to cover herself as his gaze slowly slid up her body like a lover's caress. When his eyes met hers, the appreciation she saw in the dark brown depths sent her pulse racing and caused her breathing to become all but nonexistent.

"You're absolutely beautiful, Katie." He quickly

worked his belt through the metal buckle. "I don't ever want to hear you say otherwise."

Before she could respond, he released the snap at his waistband and made quick work of the fly. Fascinated, she watched as Jeremiah shoved his jeans and white cotton briefs down his long, powerful legs, then kicked them out of the way.

Starting at his feet, she let her gaze drift upward. She noticed a fairly new surgical scar on his left knee and an older, faded scar on his right thigh. But before she could ask how he'd gotten the marks marring his remarkable body, her breath caught and her heart skittered to a complete halt before it took off at a gallop.

The only other nude males she'd ever seen were either babies or anatomical pictures in textbooks and encyclopedias. Not exactly an accurate representation of the adult nude male. But then, Katie had a feeling nothing could have prepared her for the reality of Jeremiah Gunn. With lean, well-toned flanks, his sex heavy and proud, he was magnificently male, impressively aroused and thoroughly…intimidating.

Looking up into his eyes, she swallowed hard. The raw hunger in the chocolate-brown depths sent a shiver straight up her spine, and for the second time since making the decision to meet his requirements, Katie had doubts about her decision.

"I'm just a man like any other, Katie," he said, apparently sensing her apprehension.

She somehow doubted that was the case. But she

couldn't tell him that. If she did, she'd give away her lack of experience.

"Your body was made to hold mine," he said, his deep voice gentle and reassuring. "We'll fit together perfectly."

Taking a deep breath, she came to the conclusion there was no turning back. She wanted a baby—more precisely Jeremiah Gunn's baby—and she'd do whatever it took to have her child. Even if it meant he'd learn that she was a thirty-four-year-old virgin.

"I haven't—"

"It's been a long time, hasn't it?"

"You could say that." More like never, but if she told him that he'd probably think she was some kind of oddity and might even back out of helping her conceive.

He chuckled. "It's like riding a bicycle, honey. Once you've made love you never forget how it's done."

"It's not really a matter of forgetting," she said cautiously. "I'm just not sure I'm any good at it."

"I'm betting you are," he said, sounding more confident than she felt. "Since it's been a while, I know you'll be tight." He took her into his arms. "But I promise we'll go slow and give you time to adjust."

His comforting words, the feel of hair-roughened male flesh against her smooth feminine skin and the insistence of his strong arousal pressed to her lower belly caused her apprehension to disappear like a mist under the warm summer sun. Heat streaked from every part of her to gather in a deliciously tight coil at the very core of her, and Katie wasn't sure how much more she could take before her knees were no longer able to support her.

"Let's get into bed, honey," he said, kissing the hollow below her ear.

All things considered, she should probably be scared witless. But the desire in Jeremiah's eyes, his gentle touch and tender smile reassured her further. She quickly came to the conclusion that she'd probably follow him over Piney Falls if that's where he led her.

Once they were lying face-to-face in the middle of his king-size bed, he brushed a strand of hair from her cheek. "You have no idea how beautiful you are, do you, Katie?"

"I've never thought of myself that way," she said, honestly.

"You are." He pulled her to him. "And I don't ever want to hear you say you're too tall or overweight. You got that?" When she nodded, he pressed his lower body to hers. "Feel how hard I am, honey? I don't get that way over just any woman."

He kissed her and the feel of his firm male lips on hers sent heat flowing all the way to her soul. Forgetting her insecurities, Katie gave herself up to the warmth of Jeremiah's embrace and every cell of her being sparkled to sensuous life.

When he cupped her breast, the friction of his calloused palm teasing her nipple sent a tingling excitement racing through her and caused a delicious tightening deep within her womb. Her moan of pleasure seemed to encourage him, and when he chafed the sensitive peak with his thumb, a shiver of pleasure rippled the length of her spine.

"Does that feel good, Katie?" he asked, turning her to her back. He nibbled tiny kisses to the rapidly fluttering pulse at the base of her throat. "Do you want me to do more?"

"Y-yes."

At the same time he slid his hand along her ribs to her waist, then the flare of her hip, he kissed his way from her collarbone down the slope of her breast to the puckered tip. Her pulse raced and the tightening in her lower belly quickly turned into an empty ache when he took the peak into his mouth to tease the sensitive nub with his tongue.

Caught up in the feel of Jeremiah's mouth on her sensitive flesh, Katie wasn't prepared for the intense sensation of having him touch her intimately. Shamelessly arching into his hand, she moaned as waves of pleasure coursed through her.

"Do you like that, honey?"

"Please—"

His hand stilled. "Do you want me to stop, Katie?"

''N-no.''

When he parted her to stroke the tiny nub of intense sensations, she closed her eyes as tremors of need touched every part of her. But when he slipped his finger inside to test her readiness, she bucked against his hand and brokenly whispered his name.

''I need—''

''What do you need, Katie?'' he asked as he continued to excite her with a tenderness that brought tears to her eyes.

Unsure of exactly what she needed, she moved her legs restlessly in an effort to ease the building pressure in her feminine core. ''Please—''

''Do you want me inside of you, Katie?''

''Yes.''

''Now?''

Opening her eyes, her gaze met his and the hunger she saw in the chocolate-brown depths stole her breath. ''P-please, Jeremiah…''

But when he parted her legs with his knee, her voice trailed off and she went perfectly still.

Apparently sensing the change in her, he smiled as he moved over her. ''Just relax, honey.''

When she felt his strong arousal nestled against her thighs, she scrunched her eyes shut, held her breath and tried not to think about the pain she knew was inevitable.

''Katie, look at me.''

She opened first one eye, then the other to stare up at Jeremiah's handsome face. He was frowning.

"You're not afraid of me, are you?"

She shook her head. "I'm just feeling a little...vulnerable. That's all."

The appearance of his tender smile caused her heart to flutter. "Do you trust me, honey?"

"Yes." She had no real basis for her confidence in his integrity, but she somehow knew his honor was above reproach.

"Good." His lips brushed over hers in a soft kiss. "You have my word that I'll never hurt you, honey."

She knew better, but instead of telling him that, she forced a smile as she wrapped her arms around his wide shoulders. "Make love to me, Jeremiah."

"It will be my pleasure." He guided himself to her. "But only after I've made sure it's yours, too."

Lowering his mouth to hers, Jeremiah kissed her as he eased his hips forward. He wanted to give Katie's body time to adjust to his since it had been a while for her. But as he slowly pushed forward he met a resistance that could only mean one thing—he was venturing where no man had gone before.

He froze. "This is your first time, isn't it?" he asked, raising his head to stare down at her.

Apprehension filled her blue-green eyes as she nodded. "Y-yes."

A feeling he couldn't begin to describe touched him all the way to his soul. He'd never made love to a virgin before. In fact, he wasn't sure he'd ever known one.

"Why didn't you tell me?" he asked, his voice sounding more harsh than he intended. He wasn't as angry as he was frustrated that she hadn't trusted him enough to tell him.

"I wasn't sure...that is, I thought you might not—"

"You were frightened that I would back out of our agreement, weren't you?" he guessed, making sure to soften his voice to a more reasonable tone.

"Yes." She looked so damned vulnerable his chest constricted painfully.

"I knew having a child was important to you, but I didn't realize how much, honey," he said, wiping a lone tear from the corner of her eye. "I'm just glad I found out in time to keep from hurting you more than I'll have to when I take your virginity."

She looked surprised. "You're still going to help me have a baby?"

"I gave you my word, didn't I?"

She nodded. "I'm sorry I didn't realize it wouldn't matter."

"Oh, it matters. A hell of a lot. But not in the way you think it does." He eased his hips back, then forward. "This is a first for me, too." At her look of confusion, he smiled. "You've never made love, and I've never taken a woman's virtue."

Tracing her perfect lips with his tongue, he continued the slow rocking motion, hoping that what he was doing would ready her for what was to come. She was new to lovemaking and needed time to get used to his invasion. But never in all of his thirty-seven years had he experienced such an all-consuming need to claim a woman as he did with Katie. And he was having a hell of a time holding himself in check.

Jeremiah waited until he felt her begin to relax around him. Then, as he deepened the kiss, he pushed his lower body forward until the thin barrier gave way and he felt himself completely buried inside of her.

Her shocked gasp against his mouth caused his heart to stall, then pound against his ribs. She'd just given him a gift that she could only give once, and even though he knew she'd done it in order to have a baby, he still felt humbled by the fact that she'd chosen him to be the man to take her virginity.

"Breathe deep and try to relax," he said when he broke the kiss. He wanted to make her first time as easy as possible, but he wasn't quite sure how to do that. His hand shaking slightly, he stroked her silky, dark brown hair as he gazed down at her pretty face. "The discomfort should ease in just a minute or two, honey."

"It's not…as uncomfortable…as I thought it would be," she said, sounding as if air was in short supply. "I just feel…so full."

Buried inside of her the way he was, his muscles strained to complete the act of loving her, but Jeremiah ignored them. He wasn't about to give into his own lust before he was assured that Katie was past the pain and ready for him to give her pleasure.

"I promise this is the only time I'll hurt you, Katie," he said, kissing her forehead. "From now on when I love you, it's only going to feel good."

As he gazed down at her, he waited until he detected the acceptance in her pretty eyes, felt the tightness surrounding him ease. Then, slowly, carefully he began to move and closing his eyes, he concentrated on maintaining his control. Flickers of light danced behind his eyelids from the strain of holding himself back, but he refused to let go. Katie was trusting him to make her first time as easy as possible and he'd be damned if he let her down.

But when she started to respond to his lovemaking, her body meeting his halfway, he opened his eyes to find a need in the depths of her aqua gaze that matched his own. Quickening his pace, he watched her cheeks begin to glow with passion, felt her feminine inner muscles tighten around him as she climbed toward the pinnacle.

"That's it, honey," he rasped out. "Just let it happen."

When her nails suddenly pressed into his skin and she moaned his name, he knew she was almost there. Holding her close, he deepened his rhythmic thrusts and felt the tension within her shatter as she found her release. Her climax triggered his own, and shuddering from the force of it, Jeremiah held back nothing when he filled her with his essence.

Seven

His energy completely spent, Jeremiah buried his face in Katie's shoulder as he tried to catch his breath and come to terms with what had just happened. Nothing in his past experience could have prepared him for the intensity of making love with her. Never had the feelings been quite as keen, the need to bring a woman pleasure as strong.

He took a deep breath, trying to force some much needed air into his lungs. "Are you all right, honey?"

"Yes," she whispered.

Something in the sound of her soft answer had him raising his head. His heart stalled when he noticed tears clinging to her long, dark lashes.

"What is it, honey? Did I hurt you that much?"

Shaking her head, she gave him a watery smile. "That was more beautiful than I ever imagined it would be. Thank you."

Relieved to know that she was all right, he rolled to her side, then gathered her to him. "I should be the one thanking you, honey."

"Why?" She looked confused.

"You allowed me to be the first man to touch you, to make love to you." He pressed a kiss to her forehead. "Thank you for trusting me."

She was quiet for several long moments before she spoke again. "Do you think I'll get pregnant tonight?"

He couldn't believe the pang of disappointment that coursed through him at her question. He'd felt a deeper connection with her than he'd ever felt with any woman he'd made love with, and all she could think about was whether she'd gotten pregnant?

But as he lay there thinking about it, he couldn't help but wonder if he might not have lost his mind. How had he let himself forget that their coming together was for no other reason than making her pregnant? He wasn't interested in making an emotional connection with Katie or any other woman. Ever.

"I'm not sure," he said, mentally shrugging off his disturbing introspection. Turning her to her back, he leaned down and kissed her long and hard. "But you

know what they say, honey. If at first you don't suc-
ceed, try, try again.''

"But how…do we know…we weren't already successful?'' she asked, sounding as if she'd run a mar-
athon.

"We don't,'' he said, pressing his rapidly harden-
ing body to her thigh. "But it never hurts to have a
little insurance.''

Her eyes widened. "But the book said—''

He put his index finger to her lips to cut her off.
"Forget the damn book.'' He ran his hands over her
soft, feminine skin, feeling her body begin to warm
from his touch. "Did you enjoy making love with me,
Katie?''

The blush on her cheeks deepened and she nibbled
on her lower lip a moment before she nodded.

"Then what do you say we relax and let nature
take its course?''

"Do you think that will work?'' she asked, smiling
as she put her arms around his neck.

"Sure thing, honey.'' He kissed her until they both
gasped for breath, then moving over her again, he
slowly entered her welcoming body.

The look of ecstasy on her face was one he knew
he'd never forget. "Well, if you're sure,'' she said,
smiling.

"I am. And while nature is doing its thing…'' He
grinned as he pulled his hips back, then moved them
forward. "…we'll be doing ours.''

* * *

"Hey in there, anybody at home?"

Katie jerked awake. Who was yelling outside and why? Harv was the only one who visited Jeremiah on a semiregular basis. But hadn't Jeremiah told him that he'd be busy for the entire weekend?

When she heard Jeremiah's succinct curse, followed by the sound of the door slamming as he stepped out onto the porch to see what the man wanted, she smiled. It sounded like Jeremiah would be sending Harv on his way in nothing flat.

Stretching, she noticed her body was a little tender and had several curious minor aches, reminding her of what she and Jeremiah had shared. They'd made love twice before drifting off to sleep in each other's arms, then he'd awakened her sometime during the night to love her again.

But when she thought of their lovemaking this afternoon, her cheeks grew warm and she bit her lower lip to keep an embarrassed giggle from escaping. The man was insatiable. They'd been sitting on the couch discussing the differences between fly-casting and spin-casting when he'd taken her into his arms. Before she knew what was happening, he'd picked her up as if she weighed nothing at all and carried her into the bedroom.

She sighed contentedly as she threw back the covers, and wrapping the sheet around her, got out of bed. Jeremiah had been so gentle and considerate—

making sure she didn't experience any discomfort, assuring her pleasure before he found his own. And he'd taught her things about her own body, had drawn responses from her, that she'd never in a million years have dreamed possible.

When she walked down the short hall, she stopped to stare at the mirror on the back of the bathroom door. How could she look the same when so much about her had changed in the past couple of days?

She was still almost six feet tall and fifty pounds overweight. But it didn't matter anymore. Jeremiah had taught her that size had nothing to do with a woman being desirable or sensuous.

Her heart swelled with an emotion she couldn't begin to describe. He'd made her feel cherished for the first time in her life and she was having to fight to keep her feelings for him under control. Although the attraction between them was undeniable, and their lovemaking more incredible than she could have ever imagined, she had to remember that he wasn't looking for a woman in his life, nor was she looking for a man. She wasn't spending time with him because of any romantic inclinations they had toward each other. They'd made an arrangement to have a child together. Period. But that didn't keep her from wishing things could be different.

Placing her hand on her stomach, she couldn't help but wonder if they'd been successful. Had they already accomplished their goal? Could she have conceived her child—their child—last night or this afternoon?

"Katie?"

When she turned at the sound of Jeremiah's voice, her smile faded. He looked anything but happy.

"What's wrong?" she asked cautiously.

He walked over to stand in front of her. "Your brother is here."

"That was Alex a few minutes ago?" She covered her mouth with her hand to stifle her startled gasp. "How did he know where to find me?"

Jeremiah's mouth flattened into a tight, disapproving line. "Do you have to ask?"

Katie shook her head. "Sadie."

He nodded. "Your brother went by Harv and Sadie's place when he discovered you weren't home. Naturally, Sadie had a theory where you might be and sent him here."

"But why would Alex drive all the way down here from Virginia?" she wondered aloud. "He hasn't been back home for a visit since he was here at Christmastime two years ago."

"I don't know why he's here, honey. But you'd better get dressed. He wants to talk to you, and even though I think you look cute as hell, I doubt he'd be all that amused to see you wearing nothing but a bed sheet." Jeremiah cupped her cheeks with his palms, then gave her a quick kiss. "Don't worry. You aren't going to have to face him alone. We're in this together. Remember?"

"Thank you," she said, wondering why she felt more like an insubordinate teenager than a thirty-four-year-old woman who had just come into her own. "Tell Alex I'll be right out." As Jeremiah started to go back out onto the porch, she asked, "Is Harv with him?"

Turning, Jeremiah shook his head. "Alex said Harv was too busy trying to find somebody to guide a fishing party on Piney River tomorrow, while he took another couple of guys out on Little River."

"I suppose we can be thankful for small favors." When Jeremiah raised a dark eyebrow, Katie shrugged. "At least we won't have the benefit of an audience if spit hits the fan."

"It's so good to see you again," Katie said, hugging her brother. Alex was only a year older than her, and they'd always been close.

"I've missed you, Katie-did," Alex said, using the nickname he'd given her when they were children. "How have you been?"

"I've been fine," she said, genuinely glad to see him. "But why didn't you tell me you were coming home for a visit?"

To his credit, her brother looked chagrined. "I didn't even know it myself until late last night when Mom called and got me out of bed." He sighed heavily. "I tried to talk her out of it, but she insisted that I drive down here and find out just who it was you're carrying on with, and how serious you are about him."

Unsure of how to respond to Alex's reason for being there, she glanced over at Jeremiah sitting on the swing.

Without hesitation, Jeremiah held out his hand for her to join him. "Katie and I have just recently started seeing each other," he said. "So it's really too soon to tell where things will go with us."

Grateful for his diplomacy, Katie sat down beside him. When he put his arm around her shoulders and pulled her to his side, she noticed Alex raise an eyebrow.

"So what did Sadie tell Mom?" Katie asked, redirecting the focus back to the matter at hand.

"To tell you the truth, I'm not real sure," Alex said, sounding extremely tired as he sat on the bench opposite the swing. "Mom was a little upset. But she mentioned something about you and a stranger, then something else about a motorcycle." He ran an agitated hand through his thick, dark brown hair. "I tried to tell her that you're old enough to know what you're doing, but she wouldn't listen. Apparently Sadie really laid it on thick about no one knowing much about Jeremiah."

"No telling what Sadie told her," Katie said, her anger rapidly reaching the boiling point. It bothered her that the woman had upset her mother and that it had ultimately inconvenienced her brother. "I wish that woman would learn to mind her own business."

"I think we both know that's never going to happen," Alex said, shaking his head. "But in all fairness to Sadie, Mom did tell her to watch out for you when she and Dad moved out to California to help Carol Ann."

"Yes, but I'm not a teenager," Katie said, feeling more frustrated by the second. "I'm a grown woman and I'm perfectly capable of making my own decisions. I don't need the town busybody reporting my every move to my mother."

Alex held up his hands in surrender. "I don't think it would have bothered Mom nearly as much if she'd been able to get hold of you last night," Alex said, clearly trying to placate her. "But it was midnight when she tried to call and it shook her up pretty good when you weren't home."

Katie released a resigned sigh. "I'm sorry Mom was worried. But I'm thirty-four years old. I don't need a curfew, nor do I need to explain why I wasn't home." She sighed heavily. "And sending my brother over five hundred miles to check up on me was just plain ridiculous."

Jeremiah had listened to the exchange between Katie and her brother, and one thing was very apparent. Katie had a family who loved her dearly, and their concern for her well-being was understandable. It was something he'd never had, but that didn't keep him from recognizing it when he saw it.

"Your mother was only wanting the assurance that you're all right, honey." He kissed her soft cheek, then met Alex's deep blue gaze head-on. "Katie spent the night here with me."

"That's what I figured," Alex said, his gaze never wavering from Jeremiah's.

Unless Jeremiah missed his guess, he and Katie's brother would be having a talk in the not too distant future about Jeremiah's intentions toward her. "Katie, your brother looks like he needs a drink. Would you mind getting us both a beer out of the fridge?"

She gave him a curious look, then rising from the swing she started toward the door. "Would either of you like anything else?"

"No," Jeremiah and Alex both said at the same time.

They continued to stare at each other until Katie had gone inside the cabin. "How would you like to go fishing tomorrow morning, Alex?" Jeremiah asked. "I'm betting you want to talk to me without Katie hearing what you have to say."

The man nodded. "You got that right."

"How does six o'clock sound?" Jeremiah asked.

"Early," Alex said with a grunt.

Jeremiah laughed. "Katie said you live in Virginia. That's a long drive and I'm betting you're ready to drop in your tracks."

Alex nodded. "Driving from Alexandria is a good distance from here."

"Alex works in D.C.," Katie said, walking back out onto the porch.

Jeremiah took the aluminum can she offered him. "I know the area well. I was stationed at Quantico a few years back."

Alex took a swig of his beer. "You're a marine?"

"Was," Jeremiah said, shaking his head. He put his arm around Katie's shoulders when she sat back down beside him. "I was discharged two months ago after I tore up my knee on a mission."

"Is that the reason for the scar on your left knee?" Katie asked. He watched her cheeks color when she realized she'd just admitted to seeing him without his pants. He smiled. She always looked so damn sweet and tempting when she blushed.

"I had to have some of the cartilage removed and my anterior cruciate ligament repaired," he said, waiting for the pang of regret that always accompanied his thinking about the end of his military career. It surprised him that his sense of loss wasn't quite as keen as it had been in the past.

"Well, if we're going fishing tomorrow morning, I've got to get some rest," Alex said, yawning. "I haven't slept since night before last."

Katie frowned. "But I thought you said Mom got you out of bed when she called last night."

Jeremiah laughed out loud at Alex's sheepish grin.

"Honey, your brother said he was in bed. He didn't say anything about sleeping."

He watched the blush on her cheeks deepen when it dawned on her what he meant. Jeremiah didn't think he'd ever seen her look so pretty.

She shook her head. "Never mind."

Grinning, Alex stood up and stretched. "Katie-did, could I borrow your keys to the house? I left mine at my condo."

"Of course." Katie rose from the swing. "I'll get them for you."

After Katie went inside to get the keys to their parents' house, Jeremiah got to his feet. "You do know Katie will be staying here with me?"

Alex nodded. "I figured as much."

"You don't have a problem with that?" Jeremiah asked.

"I'll let you know after our fishing trip tomorrow," Alex said grinning.

Katie stopped slicing tomatoes to stare at Jeremiah, open-mouthed. "You didn't."

"Sure did." Jeremiah nodded as he switched off the stove. "I just told him that you would be spending the night with me."

Closing her eyes, she shook her head. "I can't believe how out of control everything has become."

"What do you mean?" he asked, placing the trout

he'd been frying for their supper on two plates. "I thought everything was going pretty well."

She shook her head. "In less than twenty-four hours, I've given the local gossips more than enough fuel to keep the rumor mill running for months, worried my mother half to death simply because I finally got a life and had something else to do besides stay at home on a Friday night, and now my brother is home for the first time in two years, just to check up on me." She took a deep breath. "That's not just out of control. It's downright chaotic. And all because I wanted a baby before it's too late."

He set the skillet he'd been using on the back burner of the stove, took the knife and partially sliced tomato out of her hands, then took her into his arms. "Honey, gossips are always going to talk. You know that. You and Alex called your mother and assured her that everything is fine before he left." Jeremiah's lips brushed hers. "And with Alex staying at your place there's nothing keeping us from making love."

"But—"

"Alex won't be back until tomorrow morning." Jeremiah's promising grin caused her insides to quiver and her knees to go weak.

Leaning close, he whispered what he had in mind and Katie felt as if her whole body blushed. "We can't do that."

"Honey, we can do anything we damn well please," he said, tickling the sensitive skin below her ear with his tongue. ''And I'm going to enjoy the hell out of showing you how much you'll like it when we do.''

Shivers of anticipation skipped up her spine. ''But what about—''

''Forget about getting pregnant and just enjoy what I do to you,'' he said, sealing his mouth over hers in a kiss that caused her head to spin.

''In other words, let nature take its course,'' she said, repeating what he'd told her last night.

When he pressed his lower body close to hers, grinned and kissed her again, she forgot all about the purpose of their weekend together. All that seemed to matter was being in the arms of the man who was quickly becoming as important to her as the air she breathed. Her pulse raced and if he'd given her time, the realization might have scared her witless. But as he moved against her, an answering rhythm like a sultry jungle beat thrummed through her veins. She was lost to anything but the way Jeremiah was making her feel.

Breaking the kiss, he took her by the hand and started down the hall. ''Right now nature's set a course that I fully intend to follow to its completion.''

''What about dinner?'' she asked, laughing when he stopped to swing her up into his arms.

He grinned. ''We'll heat it later in the microwave, *if* we have enough strength left to get out of bed.''

When they entered the bedroom, he kicked the door

shut behind them, then set her on her feet. "Let's get these clothes out of the way," he said at the same time he lifted the hem of her blue T-shirt.

In no time, he had them both stripped. Leading her over to the bed, he waited until she pulled the comforter back and lay down. Stretching out beside her, he took her into his arms and kissed her with a tenderness that left her breathless.

Every cell in her being sparked to life as Jeremiah parted her lips and once again explored her inner recesses. But when he used his tongue to imitate a more intimate coupling, flickers of light danced behind her closed eyes and the blood in her veins felt as if it had been replaced with liquid fire.

As he continued to tease her, he slid his hand over her abdomen, then up to cup her full breast. He brushed his thumb over her hardened nipple and Katie felt a spark of excitement ignite within her soul. But the delicious feelings reached a new level when he lifted his lips from hers and replaced his thumb with his mouth. Tracing lazy circles around the taut tip with his tongue, Jeremiah teased her relentlessly before taking the bead in to draw on it deeply.

Her nerves seemed charged with an electric current as he kissed his way down her abdomen to her rounded stomach. So caught up in the sensations he was creating within her, it took a moment for Katie to realize what he intended when he pressed his lips to the sensitive skin just below her navel.

"N-no, you can't," she said, sounding unconvincing even to her own ears.

His deep chuckle caused a delicious fluttering in the pit of her stomach. "Honey, I not only 'can,' I'm going to."

She shivered when he moved to kiss his way down the top of her thigh to the inside of her knee, then back up. Gripping the sheet with her fists, she couldn't stop the soft moan that escaped when he found her and carried through on the promise he'd made her earlier while they were preparing supper. Wave after wave of pleasure flowed over her as Jeremiah teased and coaxed, enticing her to new heights of passion, taking her to the brink of her own sanity.

"Please, Jeremiah."

Raising his head, he smiled. "Do you like that, Katie?"

"N-no." When he kissed her again, she couldn't seem to think or pull enough air into her lungs. "I…yes. Please…I need—"

"What do you need?" he asked, sliding his body up over hers.

Katie felt the blunt tip of him against her most feminine part as he stared down at her, awaiting her answer. "I…need…you."

"Where do you need me, Katie?" he asked as he brushed a strand of hair from her cheek.

"I-Inside," she gasped when he moved ever so slightly against her.

"Was I right about you enjoying it when I brought you pleasure this way?" he asked softly.

"Yes." If he didn't do something soon, she was sure she would burst into flames.

It felt as if fireworks ignited in her soul when Jeremiah gathered her into his arms to join their bodies in one smooth stroke. Setting a slow, leisurely pace, he seemed mindful that her body was tender from their lovemaking, and Katie could no longer deny that she was falling head over heels for him.

If she'd been able to think, she'd probably have panicked at the realization. But the tension he was building within her was rapidly reaching a crescendo, and she was lost to anything but the multitude of sensations enveloping her.

He must have sensed her need for release because he deepened his thrusts and the tight coil of need inside her suddenly broke free to send a delicious wave of heat flowing throughout her body. Stars flashed behind her closed eyes and she felt as if their souls united as he took her to a place only lovers go. She felt his big body go perfectly still a moment before he called her name, and joining her in the vortex, found his own liberation from the exquisite storm.

When he collapsed on top of her, she wrapped her arms around his shoulders and held him close as emotions she wasn't ready to deal with overtook her. How could he have come to mean so much to her in such a short time?

She'd known from the beginning that they were only spending time together in order for her to conceive a baby. Why had she allowed herself to develop feelings for him?

Katie bit her lower lip and willed herself to remain calm. She'd played a dangerous game when she agreed to Jeremiah's terms, and she had a feeling he'd taken more than her virginity when he'd taken her to his bed.

She had a feeling that somewhere along the way he'd taken her heart as well.

Eight

Jeremiah whipped the fly rod in his hand back and forth several times in order to lengthen the line before he allowed the Wooly Bugger fly he'd tied to the nylon leader at the end of the orange cord to touch the water upstream. He watched Alex do the same from several feet away, and in no time they'd each landed a nice-size trout. He caught Alex eyeing him several times as they played a cat-and-mouse game with the fish, but Alex made no move to wade over to try to talk to him.

"I've got my limit," Alex finally said, slowly moving through the water toward Jeremiah. He hooked his thumb toward the remnants of a fallen tree laying on the water's edge. "What do you say we sit and talk a while?"

Jeremiah wound in his line and followed Alex over to the stream bank. He had a good idea what Alex was going to ask him, but Jeremiah wasn't sure how he was going to answer.

He wasn't going to lie to the man and tell him that he and Katie were planning a lasting relationship. They weren't—at least not beyond their having a child together. But he couldn't deny that he had feelings for Katie, either.

Somehow, she'd managed to get under his skin without him realizing quite how it happened, and in the past couple of days, he'd even been giving serious thought to making his move to Dixie Ridge permanent. If they were successful in making her pregnant, it would be where his only blood relative lived. Besides, he had to call somewhere home now that he wasn't moving around at the whim of the Marine Corps.

Deciding that strategically it would be to his advantage to take the offensive, Jeremiah sat down on the fallen log and started dismantling his fly rod. "I'm betting you want to know how serious things are between me and your sister," he said, placing the sections into a carrying case.

"It's crossed my mind," Alex said as he took apart the fishing rod Jeremiah had loaned him.

"I can't honestly tell you anything beyond the fact

that I have the utmost respect and admiration for Katie." Jeremiah stared at the water rushing over the rocks in the stream bed. "She's special."

Alex closed the case holding the pieces of fishing rod. "As Katie pointed out last night, she's old enough to make her own choices. And I agree. She's not a kid who has no idea what she wants. She's a grown woman with a mind and will of her own." He looked Jeremiah square in the eye. "But I'm telling you right now, I don't want to see her hurt."

"I can understand your concerns," Jeremiah said, nodding. "But let me assure you, I have no intention of doing anything that would harm or upset your sister in any way. Like I said, she's special."

Alex tossed a pebble into the water. "She's not that experienced with men."

Jeremiah nodded. "I figured that out the first time we talked."

"Since people haven't seen Katie dating a whole lot, you do realize that the two of you are the talk of Dixie Ridge right now," Alex added.

"That's the biggest drawback of a small town." A knot formed in Jeremiah's stomach every time he thought of someone maligning Katie. "Everybody knows your business."

"Tell me about it. That's the main reason I took a job away from here," Alex said, clearly disgusted. "I got tired of people talking about—"

When he stopped abruptly, Jeremiah gave him a

curious glance. Alex looked as if he was remembering something he'd rather forget. But Jeremiah wasn't about to pry. He had things in his own past he didn't care to discuss.

"Anyway, I have no doubt Katie can handle whatever they have to say," Alex finally said.

Jeremiah rose to slip off the waist-high rubber waders. "They can say what the hell they want to about me. But I'd better not hear anyone say a word against Katie."

"They're going to talk, no matter what you do." Alex shrugged. "If not about you and Katie, then they'll find someone else."

"In other words, some other sorry soul gets a reprieve while Katie and I are the flavor of the month," Jeremiah said, grinning.

Laughing, Alex stood up to remove the waders Jeremiah had loaned him. "That's about the size of it." When he started gathering the fishing equipment, his expression turned serious. "All I'm asking of you is that you don't hurt Katie. She's one of the strongest, most capable women I know. But, like I said, she's not all that experienced with relationships."

"You know, that's something that doesn't make a bit of sense to me," Jeremiah said as they started down the path to the cabin. "What the hell's wrong with these mountain boys anyway? Are they blind? Katie's intelligent, witty and a damn fine-looking woman." He shook his head. "Any one of them would be lucky to have her give them the time of day.''

Alex stopped to give him a wide grin. "I like you, Gunn. I think you're going to be good for Katie." When they reached the shed where Jeremiah stored his fishing equipment, his expression turned serious. "But as her big brother, I think it's only fair to warn you. Hurt my sister and I'll make the eight hour drive back down just for the pleasure of kicking your ass."

"You don't have to worry about that happening." Jeremiah stored the equipment, then closing the shed's door, he turned to face the man. "But if I did hurt Katie, I'd damn well deserve a good ass-kicking."

"Helen, is the clinic's order ready yet?" Katie asked, walking over to glance into the kitchen. "Lexi's here to take lunch over to Martha and Doc."

"Hey there, Lexi," Helen called to the woman standing on the other side of the lunch counter. "Your order will be ready in a couple of minutes."

"How are the kids, Lexi?" Katie asked as she cleared away a customer's dishes. "Did they enjoy the trip to Stone Mountain?"

"They sure did. They're over at the clinic right now telling Martha all about it." Lexi laughed. "Of course, I expect she's already heard it from Ty. He was almost as excited about the trip as Matthew and Kelli."

"How old is your baby now, Lexi?" Lately, Katie found herself asking everyone about their babies. It might have been because she loved children, but she suspected it had more to do with the fact that her period was almost two weeks late.

"I can't believe it, but Jason is almost a year old already," Lexi answered, the pride in her voice unmistakable.

"Order up," Helen called through the window. "Lexi, y'all enjoy that blackberry cobbler. My Jim picked those berries himself."

"I'm sure it will be wonderful, Helen," Lexi said, waving at the cook.

Katie handed Lexi the carry-out bag, then rang up the total on the cash register. When she noticed Lexi staring at her, Katie frowned. "What?"

"Are you feeling all right, Katie? You look a bit pale."

Katie laughed. "I'm fine. I'm just a little tired, that's all."

"I'd say she oughtta be tired," Miss Millie Rogers said as she hobbled up to the counter. "When Katie ain't workin', she's been keepin' company with that new feller up on Piney Knob."

Smiling, Lexi patted the old woman on the shoulder. "There's nothing wrong with that, Miss Millie." She started for the door. "Katie, if you continue to feel tired, make an appointment with Ty."

"I will," Katie said, waving as Lexi left the café.

When Jeremiah walked up to the counter to pay his lunch ticket, Miss Millie looked up at him with a toothless grin. "Boy, you gotta let Katie get more rest at night. She's lookin' a bit peaked."

Katie almost laughed out loud at the startled look on Jeremiah's handsome face. "Now, Miss Millie, you know you're just jealous because he hasn't offered to take you for a ride on his motorcycle," Katie teased. At eighty-five, Miss Millie was Dixie Ridge's second oldest, and without a doubt, its dearest resident.

"You're danged right I'm jealous, Katie." The old woman cackled. "If I was forty years younger and had all my teeth back, I'd have this here boy so tied up in knots he wouldn't know which end was up."

Jeremiah winked at Katie. "Would you like a ride on my Harley, ma'am?"

"I better not. Katie might not like me stealin' her beau away from her." Positively beaming, Miss Millie added, "Besides, my dress might blow up around my ears and show everybody in town my new bloomers." She looked Jeremiah up and down. "But it sure is temptin' just for the chance of wrappin' my arms around a big, fine-lookin' young buck like you."

Katie laughed so hard she had tears streaming down her cheeks at the dull red flush on Jeremiah's handsome face. It was clear he didn't quite know what to think of the outspoken old lady.

"Why, Miss Millie, what would Homer say if he

heard you talking like that?'' she asked, taking pity on Jeremiah.

The old woman snorted. ''I been waitin' for that old fool to ask me to marry him for the past sixty years. Now if Homer got down on one knee, he'd never get back up.'' Turning to Jeremiah, she shook a boney finger at him. ''Don't you go doin' the same thing to Katie that Homer Parsons done to me. Sparkin' is fine for a little while, but there comes a time when you gotta fish or cut bait, boy.''

With that, Miss Millie reached up to pat Jeremiah on the arm, handed Katie the money for her lunch, then hobbled out of the café as fast as her eighty plus years would allow.

''What the hell was that all about?'' Jeremiah asked, looking more confused than ever. ''What did she mean by fish or cut bait?''

''I think it was Miss Millie's way of telling you that we should stop seeing each other if we aren't going to get married.'' Katie sighed. ''I suppose it's something we have to contend with.''

''Have others said anything?'' he asked, handing her the money for his lunch. ''What about Sadie and her crew of old biddies?''

Katie shook her head. ''If they're talking about us, I haven't heard about it.''

''I don't think you will.''

''Really?'' she asked, doubtful that would be the case.

When she handed him his change, he gave her a smile that sent her pulse racing. "The day after Alex left to go back to Virginia, Harv and I came to an agreement."

Katie stared at him. "What on earth did you tell him?"

Jeremiah shrugged. "That I didn't want to hear any gossip about us."

"What does he get out of the deal?" She knew better than to think Harv was agreeing to keep Sadie quiet without getting something in return.

"It doesn't matter," Jeremiah said, smiling. He reached across the counter to take her hand in his. "I'll be back around three to get you."

"That won't be necessary," she said, shaking her head. "I thought I'd take a nap, then drive up there later."

"Are you feeling all right?" he asked, looking concerned.

Smiling, Katie nodded. "I'm fine. I just haven't been getting a lot of sleep lately."

"Taking a nap is probably a good idea." His sexy grin caused her insides to feel as if they'd turned to warm pudding. "I doubt we'll be doing a lot of sleeping this weekend."

Jeremiah sat on the porch steps of his cabin, watching the shadows of early evening spread across the mountain. It was after supper and Katie still hadn't shown up. She should have been here hours ago. He checked his watch for the second time in as many minutes. If she didn't show up soon, he was going to ride down and see what was keeping her.

His heart suddenly thudded against his ribs like a jackhammer. When had he ever cared whether or not a woman stood him up?

But he wasn't waiting on just any woman. He was waiting on Katie and it wasn't like her to tell him she'd do something and then not carry through on it. Something had to be wrong.

An uncharacteristic emotion filled his chest—one that he hadn't felt more than a handful of times in his entire life. Fear.

In all the years that he'd served his country, he'd faced going into combat several times. And although he'd been anxious and more than a little wary a few times, he couldn't say that he'd ever experienced the degree of fear he was feeling now.

His gut twisted into a tight knot and he swallowed hard against the bile rising in his throat. What if something had happened to Katie?

Getting to his feet, Jeremiah dug in his jeans pocket for the key to his Harley, then strode purposefully over to his motorcycle. To hell with waiting around for her to show up, he was going to find her and see for himself that she was all right.

As he sat down on the leather seat, he tried not to think why he was so concerned about Katie's whereabouts and well-being, nor did he dare analyze his motives too closely. He wasn't sure he was prepared to face what he discovered about himself.

But just as he got ready to start the motorcycle, he heard a vehicle coming around the bend in the driveway. Looking up, he couldn't believe the relief that washed over him at the sight of Katie's red SUV pulling to a halt beside him.

Getting off the Harley, he marched over to the driver's door and yanking it open, asked, "Where the hell have you been?"

"What bug flew up the leg of your pants?" she asked, giving him a look that would have stopped a lesser man dead in his tracks.

But after discovering his initial fears were unfounded, Jeremiah was thoroughly ticked off that she hadn't bothered to call and let him know she'd be running late. "Dammit, Katie, you told me you'd drive up here after you got off work and took a short nap. That was over five hours ago."

"I must have been more tired than I realized," she said, shrugging one shoulder as she got out of the truck. "I slept almost four hours."

"Are you feeling all right?" He knew they'd missed a little sleep in the past few weeks, but he didn't think she should be *that* tired.

"I'm fine." She hid a yawn behind her hand. "Although, I do think I could go back to sleep."

Taking her into his arms, he held her close. He

could kick himself for not letting her get enough rest. But in the four weeks they'd been making love, he hadn't been able to get enough of her. He had an unsettling suspicion that he probably never would.

"We won't make love tonight," he said decisively.

She looked up at him, and the disappointment in her blue-green eyes just about knocked him to his knees. "But I want—"

Before he had a chance to change his mind, he shook his head. "We can worry about making a baby tomorrow morning. Tonight you're going to rest."

"I wasn't even thinking about a baby," she said, smiling shyly.

Jeremiah's chest expanded with emotion as he realized Katie hadn't mentioned having a baby in the past week. The thought that she'd been making love with him because she desired him, and not because she was trying to become pregnant, caused his pulse to beat double-time.

"Are you trying to tell me that you like making love with me, honey?" he whispered close to her ear. He smiled when he felt a shiver course through her.

She leaned back to look at him. "Before I answer that, I have something I'd like to ask you."

"Ask away."

"Why were you so upset that I was late getting here? You weren't worried about me, were you?"

"Nope," he lied. He still wasn't comfortable with how concerned he'd been when she hadn't shown up on time. But there was something about letting her know that was even more unsettling. ''Now that I've answered your question, it's your turn to answer mine.'' He kissed her until they were both in need of oxygen. ''Do you like making love with me, Katie?''

''Not at all,'' she said, shaking her head.

He grinned. ''Why don't I believe you?''

''Probably for the same reason I don't believe you weren't worried about me,'' she said, smiling sweetly.

When she pulled from his arms and started toward the front porch, he groaned. He loved the way her hips moved when she walked. But as he stood there enjoying the view, he decided it was going to take every ounce of willpower he possessed to resist making love to her.

Even though she'd assured him that she was fine, it bothered him that she was so tired lately. Was she ill? That didn't seem to be the case, but what the hell did he know?

He wasn't a doctor, nor did he pretend to know all the mysterious workings of a woman's body. He knew the basics, of course, but beyond that, he was at a loss.

As he followed Katie up the steps, he suddenly remembered what one of his married Marine buddies had once said about women. *''If you're around a woman when she's doing that monthly thing, you'll know it. They get tired and cranky as hell.''*

Figuring he knew what the problem was, Jeremiah

couldn't help but breathe a sigh of relief. If Katie was getting ready to start her period, that meant she wasn't pregnant. And if she wasn't pregnant, they'd be making love for at least another month.

He knew it was selfish of him. Their agreement had been that they'd make love until they created a baby. But he wanted more time to hold her, to love her.

He wasn't exactly sure how it had happened, but Katie had become a habit he wasn't sure he'd ever be able to break.

Nine

Opening the door to the tiny bathroom, Katie smiled at Jeremiah's deep baritone belting out the classic country song, "Rocky Top." She'd learned so many endearing things about him in the past month. One of them being he loved to sing when he took his morning shower.

"You know when I was a child, I used to substitute Piney Knob for Rocky Top when I sang the chorus of that song," she said, laughing as she moved up to the side of the shower.

"Why don't you come in here and teach me that version?" he said at the same time he threw back the curtain and pulled her into the small shower stall.

Katie yelped, but it did her no good to try to escape. She was no match for Jeremiah's strength. Besides, she was already drenched from head to toe.

Staring up at him, she asked, "I suppose there was a reason for doing this."

He grinned as he gazed down at her. "I wanted to see how you'd look." He nodded approvingly. "If I was doing the judging in a wet T-shirt contest, you'd win hands down, honey."

"Uh-huh, sure," she said, looking down at her shirt plastered to her breasts. She wrapped her arms around his waist. "I was going to be nice and ask you if you'd like bacon and eggs for breakfast, but now that you've done this…" Letting her voice trail off, she shrugged.

"I want something different this morning," he said, pulling her firmly against his nude body. He nipped at the side of her neck with his lips. "I've decided I want you for breakfast."

Heat that had nothing to do with the warm spray of water sluicing over them filled every cell in her being and she found it hard to think. "I didn't…know I was on the menu."

"Oh, yeah." He tugged at the sodden knit fabric of her shirt as he tried to dislodge it from the waistband of her jeans. "I'm going to take great joy in feasting on your delightful body."

Her laughter was cut short as pain suddenly gripped her lower stomach. Groaning, she closed her eyes and held on to Jeremiah to keep from sinking to her knees in the tiny shower.

"What's wrong, Katie?" he asked, sounding alarmed.

Groaning, she shook her head. "I'm…not…sure." Then just as suddenly as the pain hit, it was gone. "I think…I'd better get out of here," she said shakily.

"Have you ever had something like this happen before?" he asked, shutting off the water. Moving them out of the shower, he peeled her clothes off, then dried her with a fluffy towel. "Let's get you into bed."

"I'm fine," she said, wondering if the cramp was a prelude to starting her period. She bit her lower lip to keep it from trembling. When she'd discovered that she was two weeks late, she'd hoped she was pregnant. But she hadn't told Jeremiah about it. It just seemed a bit premature to assume they'd already been successful.

Shaking his head, he hustled her down the hall into the bedroom. "You're not feeling well, and you haven't been for several days."

"I've been tired, but I've felt all right," she said, watching him pull something out of his dresser drawer. "So that's where you hid my nightshirt."

"I didn't want you finding it," he said, looking worried. "Put this on, honey." While she straightened the garment, he pulled on a pair of undershorts.

"Now get into bed," he said, putting on a pair of jeans.

"But I told you I don't feel bad. It's probably just a case of premenstrual cramps." Her cheeks colored from the idea of discussing something so personal with him.

"Have you ever had it hurt as much as it did a few minutes ago?" he demanded, shrugging into a gray T-shirt.

"Well, no. But—"

"Get into bed." When she stood there wondering why she was feeling irritated by his wanting to help her, he propped his hands on his hips and glared at her. "That's an order."

Narrowing her eyes, she shook her head. "You can just stuff that marine sergeant attitude of yours back into mothballs, buster. I'm not a child and I don't intend to let you order me around like one."

In the month she'd known Jeremiah, she'd only seen him startled into speechlessness one other time—the day she'd asked him to help her have a baby. Suddenly feeling as if she was about to cry, Katie bit her lower lip to stop it from trembling and meekly got into bed.

Jeremiah stared at her for several long moments. He clearly didn't know what to make of her behavior, and truth to tell, she wasn't sure why she was acting the way she was.

The confusion clearing on his handsome face, he

rubbed the back of his neck with his hand. "Is this one of those, uh, PMS things women sometimes experience?"

"I'm…not…sure," she said, sniffing back tears. She'd had minor mood swings in the past and been mildly irritable, but it had been nothing like this. "Maybe."

"Aw, Katie, don't cry." He sat down on the bed beside her and lifted her into his arms. "It's all right. You'll feel better in a few days, honey."

Katie couldn't help it, the floodgates opened and she clung to him as she sobbed. When she finally managed to get her emotions under control, she felt drained and wanted nothing more than to go to sleep.

"I—I think…I will take that nap," she said haltingly.

When he laid her back against the pillow, his understanding smile caused the lump in her throat to grow to the size of her fist. "Maybe you'll feel better when you wake up, honey," he said, wiping the remainder of her tears away with the pads of his thumb. "If you need me, all you have to do is call for me. Okay?"

The gentleness in Jeremiah's voice and the soothing hand he ran over her hair lulled her, and even as she nodded, her eyes started to close. She wasn't sure why she was acting the way she was, but it was time to find out. First thing Monday morning, she'd call the clinic and make an appointment to see Dr. Braden.

* * *

Jeremiah watched Katie move from table to table around the Blue Bird. He didn't like the way she looked. Her normally healthy complexion was pale, and she walked slowly, as if she was hurting.

His chest tightened. If he could, he'd gladly take whatever pain she was in and deal with it himself. But he couldn't and that was frustrating the hell out of him.

They might have gotten together for him to help her have the baby she wanted so desperately, but she'd quickly become the most important person he'd ever had in his life. And if they never had a child, he didn't care just as long as he could have Katie healthy and in his life permanently.

His heart suddenly slammed against his rib cage and he had to take a deep breath to slow his pulse. If he didn't know better, he'd swear he'd fallen for her. But even as he tried to deny it, the realization began to sink into his very soul. He wanted it all—Katie, kids and a place to call home for the first time in his life.

Feeling dazed, he glanced down at his plate, then back up at the woman he loved. When had it happened? When had she stolen his heart?

As he sat there thinking it over, he had to admit that he'd probably loved her from the moment their eyes met the day he'd held the door for her to enter the diner. He'd tried to deny it, tried to tell himself that he was only interested in a no-strings attached fling with her. But he'd only been lying to himself.

"Boy, did you hear me?" Harv asked, waving his wrinkled hand in front of Jeremiah's face.

"Uh, sorry, Harv." Turning his attention on the older man sitting in front of him, Jeremiah tried to focus on what Harv had said. "No, I haven't asked Ray what he wants for the cabin."

"Well, hell, Jeremiah," Harv said disgustedly. "I kept up my end of the bargain. Sadie ain't said a word about you and Katie to anybody. And let me tell you, it's about to kill her." He stared Jeremiah square in the eye. "But it's time you stopped ridin' the fence and jumped one way or t'other." Harv pointed his forkful of mashed potatoes at him. "I've been waitin' since last week when you asked me about becomin' a partner in Piney Knob Outfitters for you to make up your mind."

Jeremiah had given it some thought and he'd come to the conclusion that he liked living on the mountain. Not only did he like the simple, unhurried lifestyle, he wanted to be with Katie and the child they might have one day.

"If I do go into partnership with you, how much is it going to cost me?" he asked, taking a bite of the roast beef he'd ordered.

Harv named a figure, then added, "That would make you an equal partner." He grinned. "And when

I retire, I'll give you first crack at buying me out and becomin' sole owner of Piney Knob Outfitters.''

"What about your boys?" Jeremiah asked. "Aren't they interested in taking over when you retire?"

"Not hardly." Harv took a sip of his iced tea and shook his head. "Both of 'em moved up to Knoxville years ago. They ain't interested in comin' back here to live in Dixie Ridge."

Jeremiah nodded. "I'll want a written agreement."

Harv nodded. "I got a lawyer in Gatlinburg who can take care of that right quick."

"As soon as he has the contract ready, let me know," Jeremiah said, feeling good about his decision. "We'll go to his office together and get things squared away."

"I'll take care of it right now," Harv said, sliding his chair back from the table. "It shouldn't take more than a few days to get this deal sealed up." Grinning, he slapped a few dollars on the table. "I'll see you later, *partner.*"

Jeremiah almost laughed out loud at the speed Harv left the café. But his smile quickly faded when he noticed Katie slumped into a chair as if she was about to collapse. If it was possible, she looked even more pale than she had just minutes ago.

He was immediately on his feet and crossing the café to kneel down in front of her. "You're in pain again, aren't you, honey?"

She stared at him a moment before nodding. "I have an appointment with Doc after I get off work."

Jeremiah checked his watch. "Not good enough, honey. I'm taking you over there now."

"I can't leave," she protested. "Helen—"

"Can handle this place alone," he said, placing his arm around Katie's waist to help her to her feet. "The worst of the lunch rush is over. Besides, your health is more important than this damn café." Helping her over to the counter, he glanced through the window into the kitchen. "Helen, you're going to have to take care of things here for the rest of the day. I'm taking Katie over to the clinic. She isn't feeling well."

The woman was out the swinging kitchen doors in less time than it took for Jeremiah to hang up the apron Katie had taken off. "Katie, what's wrong?"

"I—I'm not sure," Katie said, sounding tired. "I just feel lousy."

"Let me know how she's doing," Helen said, holding the door for them as Jeremiah ushered Katie out of the Blue Bird and across the road to the clinic.

Once he had her seated in one of the uncomfortable chairs in the waiting area, he went over to talk to the nurse Katie had called Martha. "Is there any way Katie Andrews could get in to see Dr. Braden right away? I know she has an appointment for later this afternoon, but she's not feeling at all well."

Martha walked around the reception desk and over

to where Katie sat. "You are lookin' kind of puny, Katie."

"I feel kind of puny," Katie said, nodding.

Taking hold of Katie's wrist, Martha gazed at her watch for several seconds. "Your pulse is good and strong. But I agree, you need to see Doc." Turning, she started back to the reception desk. "I'll get you back in one of the examining rooms as soon as I can."

Katie nodded. "Thanks, Martha."

"It's probably just some kind of bug going around," Jeremiah said, sitting in the chair beside her. He took her hand in his and gave it a gentle squeeze. "I'm sure everything will be fine."

Glancing over at the only other person in the waiting area, Katie gave Lydia Morgan a wan smile. She liked Lydia, but she didn't feel like talking to anyone. Fortunately, the woman was too busy with three of her six children to do more than smile back.

Katie stared down at her hands as her thoughts returned to what she knew in her heart was true. She'd waited too long to try to have a child. Doc was going to tell her there wouldn't be a baby now, or in her future.

Since the weekend she'd done a lot of thinking, and she remembered when her mother had started into the change of life. Mary Ann Andrews had gone through radical mood swings, skipped periods and, at times, cramped as if she was going to start her monthly cycle. It was the same symptoms Katie was displaying now.

Biting her lower lip to keep it from trembling, she glanced over at Jeremiah. Once they discovered there was no chance for her to conceive, there would be no need for them to continue seeing each other. The agreement had only covered getting her pregnant, it hadn't covered her falling in love with him.

The thought that she'd spend the rest of her life without him caused an emotional pain ten times worse than the occasional cramping she'd been experiencing in her lower stomach. How was she ever going to live without him?

She'd tried so hard not to form any sort of feelings for him. But he'd made it impossible. From the beginning he'd made her feel beautiful and truly cherished for the first time in her entire life. When they made love he'd been gentle and understanding, and although he'd tried to deny it, he'd worried about her.

But she wasn't naive enough to believe that meant he loved her. And the longer she continued seeing him, the harder it would be to watch him ride away on his Harley for the final time once he discovered she was no longer able to have a child.

When Martha called Lydia back to see the doctor, Katie took a deep breath and blinked back her tears. Although it was the last thing she wanted to do, she had to be the one to call a halt to their unconventional relationship. Her survival depended on it.

"Jeremiah?"

"What is it, honey?" he asked, linking their fingers together. "Are you feeling worse?"

"No, I'm fine." She had to swallow hard in order to get the words past the huge lump clogging her throat. "I've changed my mind. I...don't want a baby."

"You what?" He looked incredulous.

"You heard me," she said, doing her best to keep her voice steady. "I've changed my mind. I don't think I can handle raising a baby by myself."

He shook his head. "You won't have to. Remember? I told you I'm going to be here to help."

She stared at the floor as she told the biggest lie of her life. "I know you'd do your best, but raising a child is a huge responsibility and I don't think either of us want to be tied down that way. I'm sure you have places you'd like to go and somewhere more interesting you'd rather live than Dixie Ridge."

Her heart just about broke in two when he recoiled as if she'd slapped him. Turning loose of her hand, he stood up to pace the length of the waiting area. "So you're telling me you no longer want to see me, whether we're trying for a baby or not?"

"Correct."

She wanted nothing more than to tell him that she did want to be with him—every morning and every night for the rest of her life. But she knew she couldn't do that. Jeremiah hadn't promised her anything beyond the time it took for her to become pregnant, and to help her with raising their child.

Since that obviously wasn't going to happen, it was better to say goodbye to him now. Prolonging the inevitable would only cause her more pain and heartbreak. And she wasn't sure she'd be able to survive what she was feeling now.

"Thank you for trying to help me, but it's just as well we weren't successful," she said, gazing up at him. She could tell he was angry and confused, but in time he'd look back and be thankful that she'd ended their agreement.

"Katie, could you come on back to room two?" Martha called as she removed a file from a pocket on the wall.

"So that's it? We're just going to walk away from this and that's that?" he asked, his voice sounding more like a growl than his usual rich baritone.

"It's for the best." She stood up to go back to the examining room. "This way, when you're ready to leave Piney Knob Mountain there won't be anything holding you here. You'll have the freedom to go whenever and wherever you like." Rising on tiptoe, she kissed his lean cheek one final time. "Have a wonderful life, Jeremiah Gunn."

Turning, she walked toward the back of the clinic, her knees feeling as if they would give way at any moment. Today was, without a doubt, the worst day of her life. She'd just given up the only man she'd ever loved, and she was about to find out that her last hope of having a family was at an end.

When she was settled in the tiny room, Martha asked her questions about her symptoms, then gave Katie an odd smile as she advised her to strip from the waist down and put on an open-backed gown. Doing as she was told, Katie lay back on the examining table and focused on counting the ceiling squares as she waited for Doc. She had to do something to keep from breaking down as she awaited the devastating news.

"I hear you aren't feeling well, Katie," Dr. Braden said when he entered the room, followed closely by Martha. "What seems to be the problem?"

Why did doctors always ask a person to repeat what was wrong when they had it on the chart in their hands?

"I've started the change of life," Katie answered, resigned.

"Oh, you think so?" he asked, arranging the sheet over her knees. "What gives you the idea that it's menopause and not the early stages of pregnancy?"

Frowning, Katie raised her head from the pillow to meet his amused gaze. "Because my mother experienced the same problems when she first went into the change."

Doc smiled as he started the examination. "Because of the hormonal changes, some of the symptoms can be very similar.'' A few moments later, he pulled the sheet back down. ''Katie, your womb has started to soften. We'll run a test, but I'm sure it's going to—''

''I suppose that's like everything else,'' she said, sighing as she sat up. ''Even your internal organs get soft and saggy when they age.''

Doc laughed. ''That wasn't what I was going to say. A woman's womb softens when she's pregnant.'' Smiling, he added, ''Congratulations, Katie. You're going to have a baby.''

Ten

Determination burned at Jeremiah's gut as he rode his Harley through Dixie Ridge for the first time in two weeks. He had to see Harv and find out if it was too late to finalize their deal on the partnership in Piney Knob Outfitters. Then he needed to go home and see how his newly purchased cabin had faired in his absence. After he'd taken care of those two things, he had every intention of going after Katie.

It didn't matter that she'd said he was free to go wherever he chose. Everything he wanted in life was right here in Dixie Ridge.

Checking his watch, his smiled. It was lunchtime and Harv would be at the Blue Bird shooting the breeze with anyone he could get to sit and listen to him.

Jeremiah's smile turned to a grin. The cabin could wait. He'd check with Harv, then talk some sense into the only woman he'd ever loved.

As he steered the motorcycle into a parking space in front of the café, Jeremiah shut off the engine and got off the Harley. Walking purposefully into the Blue Bird, he looked around. He spotted Harv at his usual table, talking to another one of the other regulars.

"Is that offer still open to buy into Piney Knob Outfitters?" he asked, walking up to where Harv was seated.

"Well, would you look what the cat dragged up?" Harv grinned. "Pull up a chair, Jeremiah."

"Thanks, but I have some other things to take care of," he said, shaking his head. When Harv just continued to stare at him, Jeremiah asked again, "Is that offer still good or not?"

"It's good," Harv said, nodding. "The lawyer had the papers ready a couple of days after you high-tailed it out of here. I told him to hang on to 'em. I had a feelin' you'd be cruisin' back into town."

Jeremiah nodded. "I appreciate it, Harv. When do you want to finalize the deal?"

"How about we go first thing in the mornin'?" Grinning from ear to ear, Harv stuck his hand out. "Glad to have you as a partner, boy."

When he shook Harv's hand, Jeremiah detected movement out of the corner of his eye. Expecting to see Katie serving someone their food, he was surprised to see a teenage girl waiting tables.

Snapping the wad of chewing gum in her mouth, the little blonde walked up to him. "You staying for lunch, Mr. Gunn?"

"Not today. I just stopped by to talk to Harv." He quickly looked around the café's interior. Katie was nowhere in sight. Where was she?

"Right after you took off for parts unknown, Katie had to take some time off from workin'," Harv said as if reading Jeremiah's mind.

If Katie wasn't here to manage the Blue Bird, there had to be something terribly wrong. Dread filled Jeremiah's chest as he turned his attention back to Harv. "Is she at her place?"

Harv nodded. "Miss Millie's been stayin' with Katie since she got sick."

"What's wrong with her?" Jeremiah demanded.

"I don't rightly know what's ailin' her," Harv said, scratching his head. "When Sadie went over there to see her, all Katie would tell her is that it ain't nothin' serious."

Jeremiah had heard enough. "I've got things I need to do," he said, turning to leave. "I'll come by your house around nine in the morning and we'll go take care of getting those papers signed."

"When you see Katie, tell her I said 'hi,'" Harv called after him.

Jeremiah didn't try to deny where he was headed when he walked out of the Blue Bird and climbed on his motorcycle. As he drove it out onto the road leading toward Katie's, he berated himself for not staying in town long enough to find out what Dr. Braden had had to say about her illness. But after Katie told him she no longer wanted to see him, he'd been so disillusioned, so hurt, that he'd walked out of the clinic, gone back to the cabin to pack and left town with every intention of never setting foot on Piney Knob Mountain again.

He'd ridden over to North Carolina and ended up standing outside the gates of Camp Lejeune where his hitch with the Marine Corps had started some nineteen years ago. But he'd found that instead of lamenting the loss of his military career, all he'd been able to think about was how much he loved and missed Katie, and how her rejection had just about killed him.

He took a deep breath as he turned onto the lane leading to Katie's house. At one time or another he'd been rejected by almost everyone in his life. Even the marines had discharged him after he'd injured his knee because he was in less than perfect physical condition. But Katie's rebuff had cut a wound far deeper than he could have ever imagined.

How she'd become such an important part of his

life in such a short time was still a mystery to him. But she had, and just because she'd said she didn't want him hanging around anymore, didn't mean he'd stopped loving her.

He'd given up without a fight that day at the clinic, but he was about to change that. He needed Katie in his life as much as he needed his next breath, and he had every intention of doing whatever it took to convince her she needed him just as much.

"Miss Millie, would you please see who that is pounding on the door?" Katie asked, feeling like death would be a blessing as she dragged herself from the bathroom back to bed.

A day or two after Dr. Braden had diagnosed her pregnancy and ordered her to stay off her feet for a while, she'd started getting sick. The only trouble was, her bouts of morning sickness came in the afternoon, usually right after she'd had lunch.

A few minutes later, Miss Millie appeared at Katie's bedroom door. "It's that good-lookin' feller you was keepin' company with. He says he ain't leavin' 'til he sees you."

"Jeremiah's here?" Katie asked incredulously.

Her heart sped up. She hadn't expected to see or hear from him again. After she'd released him from their agreement that afternoon at the clinic, she'd come out of the examining room to find that he'd left. She'd called Harv to see if he knew where Jeremiah was, but all Harv seemed to know was that Jeremiah had left town that very afternoon. Katie had taken that as proof that he was relieved to once again have his freedom. And although she was devastated to think she'd never see him again, she had focused on his baby nestled safely inside of her.

"I told him to wait in the parlor while I checked to see if you was up to receivin' visitors," Miss Millie said, bringing Katie's attention back to the fact that the man she loved with all heart was waiting to see her. Miss Millie's toothless grin smoothed some of the wrinkles in her cheeks when she added, "He asked how you was, but I didn't tell him 'bout you bein' in the family way. That's your place."

"I...oh, thank you, Miss Millie. Yes, I want to talk to him." Katie reached up to brush back the strands of hair that had escaped from her ponytail and started to get out of bed. "I'll have to get out of this nightgown and put some clothes on. I'm sure I look like I've been in a train wreck."

"Well, you do look a mite peaked," Miss Millie said, nodding. "You want me to tell him to come back later?"

"No." Katie didn't want to run the risk of him not returning. No matter how relieved he'd been to leave her and Dixie Ridge behind, she needed to tell him that he was going to be a daddy. "Tell him I'll be out in a few minutes."

Miss Millie nodded. "I'll do it."

"That won't be necessary, ma'am," Jeremiah said from behind Miss Millie.

Katie and the old woman both jumped and let loose with startled cries.

"You just about scared the puddin' right out of me, boy," Miss Millie scolded. She put her hand to her chest. "Don't you know you ain't s'posed to scare an old lady like that? If my heart weren't as good as it is, I mighta dropped dead right here on Katie's floor."

"I'm sorry, ma'am," he said, giving Miss Millie a smile that Katie was sure would charm the old woman right out of her garters.

"Oh, that's all right," Miss Millie said, patting his arm. "I know you didn't mean nothin' by it." Turning to Katie, she grinned. "If you can do without me for an hour or so, I need to go by Homer's place and see how he's doin'. His arthritis has been painin' him somethin' fierce the past couple of days."

Katie knew Miss Millie was just making an excuse to give them privacy. Homer Parsons was as spry as he'd always been.

"I'll be fine," Katie assured her. "Thanks for stopping by, Miss Millie."

"I'll call in the mornin' to see if you need me to stay with you tomorrow," the old woman said. As she passed by Jeremiah, she added, "You take good care of Katie. If you don't, you'll have to answer to me, boy."

Katie watched Jeremiah's confusion turn to concern as he watched Miss Millie leave. Walking over to the bed, he asked, "You need someone staying with you all the time?"

"Not…really." Katie felt another wave of nausea beginning to build. She lay back against her pillow and closed her eyes in an effort to stop it. "Miss Millie has been so sweet and wants so much to be of help that…I don't have the heart to tell her I'd be all right on…my own."

"Are you sure of that?" he asked. "You look like you need to be in a hospital."

"I…can't…talk now."

The nausea Katie had tried to keep at bay overtook her, and throwing back the quilt, she bolted for the bathroom. She didn't have time to lock the door before sinking to her knees in front of the porcelain bowl. When she felt Jeremiah place his hand on her forehead to hold her while she was sick, then bathe her face with a damp cloth when she was finished, she could have died of embarrassment.

Tears of humiliation ran down her cheeks when he helped her to her feet. "P-Please, could you give me a moment to collect myself?"

"No." He picked her up and cradled her to his wide chest. "I'm getting you back to bed before you collapse."

Being in Jeremiah's arms again was heaven. But Katie knew better than to think he was being anything more than helpful.

Once he had her tucked back into bed, he sat on the edge of the mattress. "Is this part of what was wrong two weeks ago?" he asked, handing her a tissue to dry her eyes.

"Yes."

"What does Doc Braden have to say about this?"

"That it shouldn't last more than another month or so," she answered as she tried to think of the best way to tell him she was pregnant.

Jeremiah shook his head. "That's not acceptable. If he can't do anything for you, then we'll have to see a specialist."

"We?"

He nodded. "I'm going to make sure you get over whatever this is."

Of course he'd want to see that she was well. She'd discovered Jeremiah was a very compassionate man. But it didn't mean he wanted her back in his life.

"It's not necessary." She took a deep breath. He'd given her the perfect opening. "It's a pretty common problem for—"

"I don't care if it's common or not," he interrupted. "There has to be some kind of treatment to help you get over this."

As she gazed at the man she loved with all her heart, she had to know. "Why did you come back, Jeremiah?"

He stared at her for several long moments, before he spoke. "Because I learned something about myself the day I took you to the clinic that I never got the chance to tell you.''

''What did you learn?'' she asked, forcing herself to breathe. There was something about the tone of his voice and the light in his chocolate-brown gaze that stole her breath.

She watched him rest his forearms on his knees and loosely link his fingers between them. Staring at his hands, he spoke without looking up. ''When I came here, all I had in mind was to do a little fishing, take some time to decide what I wanted to do for a living now that I'm out of the Marine Corps, then move on.'' He raised his gaze to meet hers. ''I never expected to find you.''

''I don't think I gave you much choice.'' She arranged her pillows against the headboard in order to sit up, then leaned back against them. ''I'm the one who came to you and blurted out my request.''

''That was another thing I didn't anticipate.''

''You mean my asking you to help me have a baby?''

''Well, there was that.'' His smile sent a shiver straight up her spine. ''But until that day, I didn't want kids.''

''You didn't?''

''No.'' He reached up to rub the back of his neck as if he was searching to find the right words to explain. ''I don't have any family, or at least none that I know of. When I was five, my mother took off and left me behind for the system to take care of. I grew up in foster care and spent most of my childhood packing to move from one home to another."

"Oh, Jeremiah, I'm so sorry." Her heart broke for him. She'd grown up with the love and support of her family and friends, and couldn't begin to imagine what it must have been like for him.

"You don't miss what you've never had," he said, shrugging. "But I made a decision when I was a boy that I was never going to run the risk of having that happen to a child of mine. The only way I knew to prevent that from happening was not to have kids in the first place."

The hope she'd had that he might be happy about the baby wilted like a hothouse flower. "Then why did you agree to help me?"

"For several reasons." He took her hand in his. "I want you to hear me out before you comment, honey. Will you do that for me?"

"But—"

"I need to get this said," he insisted. "I promise you can ask me anything you want after I explain why I agreed to help you."

She wasn't sure she wanted to hear what he had to say, but she nodded anyway. "Okay. I'll listen."

"Good." Smiling, he leaned forward and pressed a quick kiss to her lips. "At first, I was trying to call your bluff, honey. I didn't really think you'd be willing to meet the conditions I set for helping you. But

I'm a man of my word, and when you agreed, I had no other choice but to go through with it.''

Jeremiah watched Katie closely as she comprehended what he was saying. He could tell what he was saying bothered her. Before she could respond, he asked, ''Do you know why I set the stipulations, Katie?''

''No.'' Her voice was so small it was almost non-existent.

''Because I wanted to scare you away.'' He shook his head. ''I never thought you'd go along with it.''

''But I did…agree to it,'' she said, her voice cracking. ''Why didn't you just try to talk your way out of it?''

''Because I'd given you my word. And…'' He paused a moment before he went on. ''…from the day you made your request, all I could think about was how much I wanted to take your beautiful body in my arms and lose myself deep inside of you.'' He took a deep breath. ''I saw your asking me to help you as serving two purposes. You'd get the baby you wanted and I'd get to make love to you with no strings attached.''

He saw the hurt in her blue-green gaze and felt like the biggest jerk that ever walked on two legs, but that couldn't be helped. She needed to know the truth about him before he told her how he felt now.

When she tried to extricate her hand from his, he lifted it to his mouth to kiss each one of her fingertips.

"But something happened when we started spending time together, Katie. The more I got to know you, the more I found myself changing my views on a lot of things. And for the first time in my life, I was somewhere I'd never been before."

She stared at him for endless seconds, her expression unreadable. "Where was that?" she finally asked.

Jeremiah took a deep breath. "I didn't plan on it—hell I didn't even see it coming—but for the first time in my life, I found myself in love."

Her eyes widened. "Y-you did?"

Nodding, he pulled her into his arms. "I discovered that I wanted to love you every night and wake up with you in my arms each morning for the rest of my life." He kissed her until they both gasped for breath. "Do you want to know the other reason I agreed to help you make a baby?"

"I'm not sure," she said, nibbling on her lower lip.

He stroked her silky brown hair. "I've always liked little kids. They're innocent and funny, and when they love, it's unconditional." He cupped her cheek with his palm and wiped away a tear with his thumb. "The thought of being a dad scared the hell out of me because I didn't know if I could be a good one. But I got used to the idea, and I trusted you not to do the same thing to our child that my mother did to me. I also knew that you'd always be there to help me be a good father."

"What if I couldn't have a baby?" she asked, her voice trembling.

He gazed at her for several long moments. "Like I told you before, you don't miss what you've never had. I'd love to have a baby with you, but if we can't, it won't change the way I feel about you."

"Oh, Jeremiah, I love you so much I ache with it," she said, throwing her arms around his shoulders.

He held her for several long moments, enjoying the feel of her body next to his. Now that he had her back in his arms, he never intended to let her go.

But something was bothering him. "Katie, if you love me, why did you send me away that day at the clinic?"

"Because I was positive I knew what Doc was going to tell me." Her lips touched the side of his neck as she spoke and his body tightened with a need that made him light-headed. She leaned back in his arms to meet his gaze head-on. "I just knew the doctor was going to tell me that I'd waited too long and would never be able to conceive."

Her reasoning was probably perfectly logical to her, but it didn't make a damn bit of sense to him. "I don't understand what that has to do with—"

"Our agreement was for us to keep trying until I became pregnant," she said, tracing her fingertip along his jaw. When her eyes met his, the love he saw in the blue-green depths caused his heart to stall. "I was afraid that once you learned that we'd never be able to have a baby, you'd leave town and I'd never see you again. And I knew the longer we were together, the harder it would be to let you go when that time came. So I gave you your freedom while I still had the strength to let you go."

His chest swelled with emotion. "You love me that much, huh?"

"More than life itself," she said, nodding.

Kissing her forehead, her eyes and the tip of her nose, he assured her, "Honey, I don't care if we never have a baby, as long as I have you."

"Really?"

He nodded. "Now what was it you wanted to tell me?"

Her smile did strange things to his insides. "I was wrong, Jeremiah."

"About what, honey?" he asked, leaning forward to kiss the satiny skin along the column of her neck.

A tremor of need coursed through Katie, but she forced herself to concentrate on what she needed to tell him. "I was wrong about not being able to have a baby. Doc said—"

"So we're still going to try after you get well?" he asked, giving her the sexiest grin she'd ever seen.

Smiling, she shook her head. "No. We aren't going to try…" When he looked disappointed, she placed her hands on his cheeks and gave him a quick kiss. "…because we've already been successful." She laughed at his incredulous expression. "We're pregnant."

He looked down at her stomach, then back up. "That's what's wrong with you?"

She nodded.

"Are you all right? What did the doctor say? Is it normal to be this sick?"

Laughing at his rapid-fire questions, she placed her finger to his lips. "Yes, I'm fine. Doc said I needed to take it easy for a few weeks because I was on my feet too much. And it's not unusual to be sick like this for the first trimester."

"Trimester?" he asked, confusion marring his handsome face. "I can see right now, I'm going to have to do some reading on this after we get married."

It was Katie's turn to give him an incredulous look. "We're getting married?"

"You bet." His grin made her insides feel as if they'd turned to warm pudding when he laid her back against the pillows, then stretched out beside her. "I'm not running the risk of you sending me away again."

"I can promise you that will never happen, Mr. Gunn," she said, kissing his lean cheek.

He captured her lips in a kiss that left her trembling. "I love you Katie Andrews. You own my heart."

Staring up into his chocolate-brown eyes, she smiled. "And I love you Jeremiah Gunn."

Epilogue

Four years later

When Katie stopped the SUV in front of the cabin, she spotted Jeremiah and their daughter seated at a child's table on the porch. Smiling, she got out of the truck and opened the back door on the driver's side of the Explorer.

As she lifted her one-year-old son from his car seat, he pointed a tiny finger toward the house. "Dada."

"That's right, sweetie. It looks like your sister has talked Daddy into having a tea party." Walking toward the porch, she hid a huge yawn behind her hand. "I see the two of you have had fun while Jacob and I were at the clinic."

Jeremiah stood up to help her up the porch steps. "Marissa insisted we had to test run her new tea set."

Katie laughed out loud. "And you do everything she tells you to?"

"Pretty much," Jeremiah said, grinning. He gave her a quick kiss as he took Jacob. "You know you've both got me right where you want me."

"And where would that be, Mr. Gunn?" Katie asked, teasingly.

"Wrapped around your little fingers." He chuckled as he turned his attention on their son. "Same as this little guy."

"I tired, Mommy," Marissa said, yawning and holding her little arms up for Katie to pick her up.

Katie lifted her little girl up to hug her close. "Did you and Daddy have fun while Jacob and I went down to visit Martha and Doc at the clinic?"

"Yes," Marissa said, smiling sleepily at Jeremiah. "Daddy eated all the chocot chip cookies."

"She kept telling me to have another one," Jeremiah said defensively.

Katie smiled. He was such a good father.

When Marissa laid her head down on Katie's shoulder, she kissed her daughter's cheek. "We'll have to make some more after you and Jacob get up from your naps."

"She's already asleep," Jeremiah said quietly. He held the door for Katie as they entered the cabin. "What did Doc Braden have to say?"

"I'll tell you about it after we get the kids down for their naps," she said, leading the way down the hall to the spare bedroom they'd turned into a nursery.

Jeremiah kissed his son and daughter, then stood beside their beds for a moment as he watched them sleep. He couldn't believe how full and rewarding his life had become since riding his Harley into town four years ago. Instead of living the life of a nomad with no one but the Marine Corps to care where he was or what he was doing, he had a beautiful wife and two of the most precious children ever, living with him in one of the greatest places in the entire world.

"You're a lucky man, Gunn," he murmured as he quietly walked out into the hall and pulled the door to the nursery almost shut.

When he went into the great room, the sight of Katie standing by the picture window looking out at the panoramic view, made him smile. It was hard to believe, but she was even more beautiful today than she'd been four years ago when he'd made her his wife.

Walking up behind her, he slipped his arms around her waist and pulled her back against him. "So how did Jacob's one year checkup go?"

"Doc said that Jacob is healthy and doing everything ahead of other children his age." She glanced over her shoulder at him. "And Martha said to tell you that Jacob looks more like you every time she sees him."

Jeremiah's chest swelled with emotion. "Thank you, honey."

"For what?"

"Everything." He nuzzled the side of her neck. "You've given me a far richer life than I ever dreamed possible."

"I'm glad you said that because it's about to get richer."

"How?" He loved the tremor of need he felt coursing through her.

Turning in his arms, she kissed his chin. "When you build that new addition on the cabin, how would you like to make it three new rooms, instead of two?"

"You've decided you want that sewing room to make your quilts, after all?"

She shook her head and gave him a smile that sent his temperature up a good five points. "No. Doc said that I'm showing no signs of going into early menopause."

"Maybe you're the exception to the rule, honey." He frowned. "But what does that have to do with my building onto the cabin?"

Her sweet smile caused his body to harden with an intensity that made him light-headed. "I can still have more children."

"Are you trying to tell me you want another baby, Katie?" He knew he was grinning like a damn fool.

But he didn't care. As long as Katie wanted babies, he was more than happy to help her make them.

To his surprise, she shook her head. "Not exactly." She cupped his face with her soft hands, then giving him a kiss that threatened to buckle his knees, she explained, "I'm trying to tell you that we've already made a baby. I'm pregnant again, big guy."

"Really?"

Yawning, she nodded.

He hadn't thought it was possible, but his happiness increased tenfold. "When are we due this time?"

"Around the first of the year," she said, yawning once again.

He chuckled. Every time Katie became pregnant it seemed as if she was sleepy through the entire first trimester. "Let's get you down for a nap."

"Will you join me?" she asked as they walked into the bedroom. "I love having you hold me while I sleep."

He couldn't have denied her if his life depended on it. "Honey, there's nothing I'd like better than holding you while you sleep."

Her impish grin sent his blood pressure off the chart. "Nothing?"

"Well, almost nothing," he said, laughing. He kissed her until they both gasped for breath. "I love you Katie Andrews Gunn."

"And I love you Jeremiah Gunn." She put her

arms around his neck. "Thank you for giving me my heart's desire."

"Honey, thank you for helping me find mine," he said as they stretched out on the bed. "You and the kids give my life more meaning than I could have ever imagined."

And as he held his beautiful wife while she slept, he knew that for the rest of their lives he'd be complete, as long as he had Katie and their babies in his arms.

* * * * *

Silhouette®

Desire®

From bestselling author

BEVERLY BARTON

Laying His Claim
(Silhouette Desire #1598)

After Kate and Trent Winston's daughter was
kidnapped, their marriage collapsed from the
trauma. Ten years later, Kate discovers that their
daughter might still be alive. Amidst their intense
search, Kate and Trent find something else they'd
lost: hot, passionate sexual chemistry. Now, can
they claim the happy ending they deserve?

THE PROTECTORS

**Ready to lay their lives on the line,
but unprepared for the power of love!**

Available August 2004 at your favorite retail outlet.

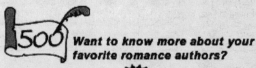

Brenda Jackson's

hottest Westmoreland title yet...

STONE COLD SURRENDER

(Silhouette Desire #1601)

Could a sky-high seduction by a tempting ingenue in the Montana wilderness change playboy Stone Westmoreland's cavalier attitude toward women...forever?

Available August 2004 at your favorite retail outlet.

COMING NEXT MONTH

#1597 STEAMY SAVANNAH NIGHTS—Sheri WhiteFeather
Dynasties: The Danforths
Bodyguard Michael Whittaker was intensely drawn to illegitimate
Danforth daughter Lea Nguyen. He knew she was keeping secrets
and Michael's paid pursuit soon spilled into voluntary overtime. They
couldn't resist the Savannah heat that burned between them, yet could
they withstand the forces that were against them?

#1598 LAYING HIS CLAIM—Beverly Barton
The Protectors
After Kate and Trent Winston's daughter was kidnapped, their marriage
collapsed from the trauma. Ten years later, Kate discovered that their
daughter might still be alive. Amidst their intense search, Kate and Trent
found something else they'd lost: hot, passionate sexual chemistry. Now,
could they claim the happy ending they deserved?

#1599 BETWEEN DUTY AND DESIRE—Leanne Banks
Mantalk
A promise to a fallen comrade had brought marine corporal
Brock Armstrong to Callie Newton's home. He'd vowed to help the
widow move on with her life, but he'd had no idea Callie would call
to him so deeply, placing Brock in the tense position between duty and
desire.

#1600 PERSUADING THE PLAYBOY KING—Kristi Gold
The Royal Wager
Playboy prince Marcel Frederic DeLoria bet his Harvard buddies
that he'd still be unattached by their tenth reunion. But when he was
unexpectedly crowned, the sweet and sexy Kate Milner entered his
kingdom. Could Kate persuade this playboy king to lose his royal wager?

#1601 STONE COLD SURRENDER—Brenda Jackson
Madison Winters was never one for a quick fling, but when she met
sexy Stone Westmoreland, the bestselling author taught the proper
schoolteacher a lesson worth learning: when it came to passion, even
the most sensible soul could lose their sensibilities.

#1602 AWAKEN TO PLEASURE—Nalini Singh
Stunningly sexy Jackson Santorini couldn't wait to call a one-on-one
conference with his former secretary, Taylor Reid. But—despite his
tender touch—Taylor was tentative to enter into a romantic liaison.
Could Jackson seduce the bedroom-shy Taylor and successfully awaken
her to pleasure?

SDCNM0704